from THE WOMEN'S PRESS

Millie Murray was born in London, in 1958, of Jamaican parentage. A qualified nurse, she has attended drama college, worked with several black theatre workshops, and been a vocalist in a gospel choir.

Her short stories have appeared in several collections including *Watchers and Seekers* (The Women's Press, 1987), *A Girl's Best Friend* (Livewire Books for Teenagers, 1987) and *Reader, I Murdered Him* (The Women's Press, 1989). She is the author of the popular teenage novel *Lady A – A Teenage DJ* (Livewire Books for Teenagers, 1989).

Kiesha
Millie Murray

Livewire Books for Teenagers
First published by The Women's Press Ltd, 1988
A member of the Namara Group
34 Great Sutton Street, London EC1V 0DX

Reprinted 1994

British Library Cataloguing-in-Publication Data
Murray, Millie
  Kiesha. ——(Livewire).
  I. Title   II. Series
  823'.914[F]

ISBN 0 7043 4129 8

Bad words and music Michael Jackson
Copyright © Mijac Music
British publisher Warner Brothers Ltd

The Way You Make Me Feel words and music
Michael Jackson
Copyright © Mijac Music
British publisher Warner Brothers Ltd

Reproduced by kind permission

Printed and bound in Great Britain by
BPC Paperbacks Ltd, Aylesbury, Bucks

I dedicate this book with love to Eugenie Saunders – my Grandmother – for her inspiration, charm and wit, Dorrel – my mother – for her strength and encouragement, and God – for blessing me with my innate talents.

Special thanks to Jan McKenley for her
patience and insight, Carole Spedding for
believing in me and giving me her time and to
all at The Women's Press – my 'extended'
family.

One

'K-i-e-s-h-a, K-i-e-s-h-a,' called Mama Tiny.

I froze. Looking in the mirror all I could see was an alien with Mum's make-up on and hair all over the place, standing in the middle of Mama Tiny's bathroom. She'll go mad if she sees me like this. I wonder what she wants.

'I'm coming,' I shouted back without opening the door.

'Yu all right chile?'

'Yes, Mama Tiny.'

'Well come nar den.'

'Okay.'

I didn't know what to do first. Should I comb my hair or should I take the make-up off? I did both. Well sort of. I combed my hair with my right hand and rubbed make-up remover over my face with my left. I had been experimenting (again) with my hair and different ways to wear Mum's make-up.

There I go, back to normal. They won't know what I've been up to. They, being Mama Tiny and Mum, were drinking tea in the kitchen.

'Waan some tea chile?' asked Mama Tiny.

'No thanks.' I grinned at her.

Mum looked at me suspiciously. 'What have you been up to then?'

'Nothing Mum,' I replied innocently. 'I, hmm, I'm going into the front room if you want me again.' I turned and walked towards the front room. I remembered how when I was much younger Mama Tiny wouldn't let me or

1

my cousins into her 'posh' front room. It was only for guests and she didn't want us kids 'mashin up me tings dem' but now that I was older I could sit still and not touch anything, so she didn't mind. I rested my head against the back of the salmon-pink plastic armchair and looked around. Never before had I really studied the contents of Mama Tiny's front room in detail, but now I felt forced to consider the various items, as soon some might be finding their way into my house!

I hope she doesn't bring those awful plastic flowers with her, I thought to myself, they look so dead! But somehow I knew, deep down inside me, the flowers were coming: no flowers – no Mama Tiny. On the mantelpiece were the usual photos of Mum and my aunts and uncles when they were children: Aunt Audrey looking like an angel with two big ribbons in her hair and Uncle Stanley in short trousers – looking at them made me laugh. On the edge of the mantelpiece was Grandfather's pipe. Mama Tiny couldn't bring herself to remove it. She would lift it up to polish underneath it and then replace it. On the coffee table in the middle of the room was an enormous vase with yet more plastic flowers and underneath the vase was a fancy doily which Mama Tiny had crocheted herself. It was pink and white, the edges stiff with starch. At least they blended in with the pink, white and red roses on the wallpaper! I slid my feet across the thick carpet – it had every colour of the rainbow in it: green, orange, red, blue, black, yellow, and I could pick out specks of white. Honestly, I don't know what Mama Tiny could have been thinking of when she bought this carpet, it must have been on special offer, or the store assistant must surely have seen her coming.

In the corner of the room behind the radiogram was Grandfather's stick. Not a walking stick, he hadn't needed one – it was a beautifully carved stick with a man's head that Uncle Stanley had brought back from Jamaica years ago as a present for him. Grandfather had really loved it, he used to run his hands over the stick, admiring the workmanship that had gone into it.

Grandfather, Grandfather. As his name came into my mind my eyes wandered across the room and settled on his photograph, taken when he first came to England from Jamaica thirty-seven years ago, after he had been married to Mama Tiny for five years. He looked right crisp in his two-piece suit. It could have been yesterday. The zoot suit which he wore then was in fashion now, and his hair, cut short except for the peak at the front, was the business. Grandfather had looked the same right up to his death. His hair, which he had kept short, had had grey streaks and he had filled out more bodily, but if you hadn't known him you would have thought he was the older brother of the man in the photo. Was it only a year ago that Grandfather had had a fatal heart attack, leaving Mama Tiny husband-less, my mum fatherless, and me grandfatherless? It had taken ages for us all to get over the death of Grandfather. He had been such a strong force in our family, his absence left a big dent.

All decisions that required serious thought or special wisdom and experience had been taken to Grandfather. I remembered the time Mum was looking for a place for us to live after Dad and she had separated and she had found a small house with three bedrooms (though the third room was really just a 'box room') and wasn't sure whether it was worth buying a three-bedroom house, because she thought a spare bedroom would be a waste. Grandfather had put her straight. 'Weell,' he drawled, 'for de present time, only yu and Kayesha' (he always pronounced my name wrong) 'live by oonoo self, but only Gaad knows' (he was a deacon in his church) 'how yur life gwine go. Yu an yur husband could patch up tings and yu ave more picknee, who know ee?' I didn't like the idea of a brother or sister but I liked the rest! 'Soo, an extra room would be a good idea.' That must've been in Mum's mind as she signed the deeds of our house.

I had liked the house as soon as I saw it. A terraced house, second from the last in the row. The front looks small, but once you get inside it is really quite big. Mum took the large front bedroom for herself, which I thought was fair enough. She had it plainly decorated in cream, with a plain beige carpet and matching curtains. Mum likes plain things, even her clothes are plain; mind you, it makes her look right sophisticated. She rarely wears snazzy clothes and she hates them brightly coloured. She nearly always has her hair tied at the back of her neck in a bun, which makes her eyes look larger than they are. Dad said that Mum's skin was the colour of Cadbury's chocolate, with the nuts in – that used to make her laugh. But what she hates is that when it's 'that time of the month' she comes out in spots! At her age. She said that Mama Tiny had had the same trouble. I hoped it wouldn't happen to me, you know these things can run in families!

My room was definitely *me*, unlike at our old house, where my bedroom was really small. I really got to hate it, with its sloping ceiling which was suffocating, it was that low. The room itself was pretty dark and in the winter, even in the daytime it was like night! The view was awful, it looked out on to an industrial estate. I had had the furniture from when I was really young: Mum had picked it – it was a boring brown with brass knobs, and I had grown as tall as the wardrobe. I couldn't even have too many pictures up on the wall as the room would be overcrowded! Now, my room in our new house was great. It had its own built-in wardrobes, giving me more space to move around, with a large mirror on the left-hand panel. I could spend hours preening and posing in front of it. I loved looking in the mirror at myself. I would try out Mum's make-up when she wasn't in (what she don't

4

know, won't hurt), putting eyeliner on my eyes, which are quite large – so people tell me – and mascara, which was waterproof – and that's true, because it was really hard to get it off! I would try out Mum's different eyeshadows and was amazed to find that gold eyeshadow really suited my cocoa-coloured skin. I looked beautiful – it's true, the mirror showed me. I loved having my hair in single extension plaits, it was really easy to manage. I could have my hair out, like Chaka Khan (which Mum wouldn't allow me to), or tie it back with ribbons of different colours to match my outfits. It really made a difference having a room of your own that made you feel *you*. I had a single bed which had another bed underneath, so that if a friend or one of my cousins wanted to stay overnight, all I had to do was pull out the spare bed instead of having them sleep in the spare room. Unless, of course, there were a few of them staying over, when the spare room it was (that bit of advice from Grandfather was a good one).

Mum had furnished the front room with furniture from a shop in Roman Road Market that imported furniture from Italy. It cost a lot of money, but she said that it was a sign of her new-found freedom from my dad.

When Mama Tiny had been told how much Mum had paid, her eyes nearly popped out of her head. 'Whaat?' she shouted, making Mum and me jump. 'Dem tief yu. Come, come we go a shop and deal wid dese people.'

'Mama Tiny, I know what I'm doing, this is exactly what I wanted and the cost is what I expected,' Mum exclaimed.

'Hmm, flea has money im buy im own dawg,' Mama Tiny huffed.

Mama Tiny didn't stay too long after that. She didn't want Mum to drop her home, so she got a cab. After she had left I asked Mum what Mama Tiny had meant about the flea buying his own dog.

'What she means,' explained Mum, 'is that money

5

doesn't make a gentleman or a lady, but it can buy almost anything. She thinks that we're becoming "posh" and she's afraid that we might be living above our means.'

'Why doesn't she just say that, instead of speaking in riddles?' I said.

'That's the way Mama Tiny is. Anyway, she worries too much and it gets on my nerves sometimes too, but I do love her and I wouldn't change her for the world . . .'

I got up out of the armchair and walked slowly around the room. I went over to the radiogram, which was old-fashioned by any standard, but Mama Tiny kept it in tiptop condition, polishing it nearly every day, and it was so shiny I could almost see myself in it. I wondered whether she was going to bring it with her to our house. I opened it and browsed through the record collection that was inside: Louis Armstrong, Fats Domino, the Lamb of God New Testament Church New York Choir. I had never heard of any of them. I took out an LP and was about to put it on when the door burst open and Patrice catapulted through it as though out of a circus cannon and managed to land on her two feet in Mama Tiny's front room.

'Hi Kiesha,' she said breathlessly. 'What's happening?'

'Well, actually,' I looked her right in the eyes, with my hands on my hips, 'I was just contemplating whether to do a double somersault, land on my hands, then turn a cartwheel and do the splits. What do you think?'

'I think you're nuts,' she laughed.

'Nuts I may be but then "nuts" is far superior to stupidity,' I said in my best Lady Di voice. Of course it was lost on Patrice.

She is my cousin and only three years my senior, but at fifteen she was such a tomboy. She had no feminine 'finesse', she was so rough in everything she did. I mean, even the way she put on her clothes, she just dragged them on, and when she took them off she slung them anywhere, usually on the floor, she just didn't care. Funnily enough, she is quite attractive. She could do so much with herself. Her black-coffee-with-a-hint-of-cream-coloured skin is so cool-looking, I don't think she'll ever need make-up – mind you, she wouldn't know how to put it on! And I have seen the way the boys look at her when she has her netball gear on: her legs are so smooth and muscular and long, it's amazing that all that belongs to someone who is not at all interested in herself.

My auntie, Mum's sister Aunt Audrey, was getting quite worried about Patrice. I heard her telling Mum that she didn't know what to do with her, but something definitely had to be done.

'Honestly, Helen, she only wants to wear trousers or jeans, she has no interest in boys and the other day she told me she wanted to do electrical engineering for her career, can you imagine? She only agreed to have her hair in extension plaits because it would save her messing around in the mornings. Oh, why can't she be like her sister Renita? She's growing into a beautiful flower, she's so feminine – a proper little lady. It's hard to believe that they're twins, they're like chalk and cheese.'

Mum sighed. Later, I heard her telling Mama Tiny on the phone about what Aunt Audrey had said about her two daughters. I could tell by what Mum was saying that it had angered Mama Tiny. Aunt Audrey was such a snob. She was forever on a diet, she lived in the hairdresser's (up the West End), having facials and her nails manicured and her hair done. I wouldn't mind, but to me she didn't look any different. She thought she looked like Diana Ross, though I heard Uncle Stanley say that she looked like a female version of Eddie Murphy, moustache and all!

They lived in Ilford, which Aunt Audrey never failed to point out was the 'green belt' and was out of London. Uncle Robin, whom she had insisted on calling Roberto ever since they had gone on a package holiday to Rome for five days, worked for British Telecom. He had a good job, but the way Aunt Audrey explained it you would have thought that he practically owned the company.

'Yes, Roberto is hardly ever at home. He is needed so much at work, I don't know how they manage without him on his days off,' she boasted.

Patrice snatched the LP out of my hand. 'Billie Holliday, God bless the child. I wish my name was Billie or something like that. Patrice is such a horrible sickly name,' she moaned.

'Don't be stupid, Patrice is a nice name. Anyway, it's not the name, it's the person who's got the problem,' I teased.

'Oi, take that back, or you'll wish you'd never been born!' said Patrice, making a lunge for me. I darted across the room and Patrice, in her haste to grab me, knocked the vase of plastic flowers off the coffee table and broke it. A pity for her, as Mama Tiny, followed by Mum and Aunt Audrey, came into the room. Patrice was bending over, picking up the pieces. 'Look how dis chile come inna mi house an mash up mi tings den ee,' said Mama Tiny, rushing over to the site of the accident and pushing Patrice out of the way.

'Sorry, Mama Tiny,' pouted Patrice out of shame.

Of course Aunt Audrey had to add her bit: 'You're so clumsy. You had better apologise to Grandmother' – she didn't like to call her Mama Tiny – 'and you can pay for the vase out of your pocket money. Go on, say you're sorry.'

'Sorry, Mama Tiny. I'll pay for your vase.'

I started to snigger.

'You can shut up, Kiesha. You're no innocent, I bet you were teasing Patrice as usual. You can pay for half of the vase from your money, now laugh at that.'

8

'Oh, Mum. It had nothing to do with me, it was all Patrice's fault, she's like a fairy elephant.'

Patrice grinned over at me and screwed up her face like a Cheshire Cat licking cream.

'Leave di picknee dem be. I ave anudda vase outside, let dem save dem money,' said Mama Tiny.

'Oh no,' said Aunt Audrey. 'Patrice has got to learn that she must respect other people's property. She's going to pay for your vase, Mother, and that's that.'

Nobody spoke. The way Aunt Audrey had said the last *that* you knew the matter was closed. I could tell from Mama Tiny's eyes and the way her mouth was going – like a cow chewing cud – that she would have liked to have said more, but she held her tongue.

Patrice and I left the adults in the front room and went into Grandfather's study. It was exactly how he had left it: his manual typewriter on the floor in the corner by the bookcase, the case for it under the table and the bookcase crammed with books of every shape, size and colour. He had about a dozen Bibles of different translations but had preferred a big dusty antique one he bought in a junk shop; he said the text was 'preserved', whatever that meant. In another corner was a Calor gas heater which Grandfather used as well as the central heating, which he thought didn't keep the room warm enough. He had an old leather Chesterfield armchair with the stuffing from the seat poking through. Mama Tiny had wanted to have it re-upholstered, but Grandfather wouldn't let her. There was a long window facing the desk which flooded the room with light. Grandfather hadn't liked the curtains drawn even at night. Mama Tiny had made a longish cushion for the window ledge so that it could be used as a seat.

There was an enormous desk, which was cluttered with papers and pens, books and old magazines; you name it, it was on the desk. He had a picture on his desk of Mama

9

Tiny when she was young – she had looked different, a bit like Aunt Audrey. Grandfather would kiss it and Mama Tiny would laugh. Mama Tiny couldn't bring herself to dismantle the desk yet, it reminded her so strongly of Grandfather and helped to keep him alive in her memory.

I sat on the low window ledge and Patrice sat in the chair at the desk, both quite lost in our own thoughts. I was thinking of Dad. Mr Lyndon Ferell, Mr Ferell. He was *so* good-looking, with large eyes (that's where I got mine from) and thick black eyelashes. His eyes were dark brown and sometimes they even looked black. He always kept his hair cropped close to his head, so it looked as though he had used tiny, tiny curlers. I remember when he grew a moustache once. It was such a contrast against his light brown skin. Mum had said she really fancied him with it. He was quite tall, with broad shoulders, which he used to put me on when I was younger, and his hands were enormous. I was glad he never really smacked me, leaving that to Mum.

Yeah, Lyndon Ferell, that's my dad. I loved him. I missed him. I wished he was still living with Mum and me. But I knew that was impossible for now. I wasn't sure how they felt about each other any more, and that made me wonder if they had ever loved each other in the first place. Well, I think they must've done, otherwise they wouldn't have got married and had me. Anyway, the pictures of Mum and Dad together before I was born were all lovey-dovey, with them looking into each other's eyes, all dreamy – there must've been something there. I don't know what had happened to turn it all so sour. I felt tears welling up inside me and a lump in my throat, threatening to cut off my air supply. I turned to look at Patrice, I didn't want her to see me crying, but she had her back to me. The tears began to fall down my face and blob off at my cheeks. I blotted them with my T-shirt, as I didn't have a tissue on me. I felt stupid crying: Mum and Dad had split

10

up a year ago, there shouldn't be any need for me to cry still. I thought of Sharon in *EastEnders*. She seemed to manage quite well after her parents had split up, in fact she was even able to take care of her mum, who was an alcoholic! Mind you, she was a couple of years older than me, but that's not the point.

I began to count on my fingers all the kids I knew whose parents had split up – Sharon Watkins, Barbie Allen, Debbie Honeywell and Beacon Wallis. I thought about them and couldn't recall anything out of the ordinary about them or their appearance, which suggested that perhaps they didn't feel too particular about their parents splitting up. Mind you, to tell the truth, Beacon Wallis was a head-case. He was definitely not the full shilling, as my Mum would say. I didn't even think he was human. He didn't have any feelings at all as far as I could see: he thought he was so hard. Once he even tried to 'locks' up his hair, but he cut it out because people laughed at him. He was such an idiot. Now he keeps his brown hair cropped. He looks as though he could be the child of mixed parents, but he isn't. He has large hazel eyes that pierce right through you – ugh! Mind you, he's quite smart and has some right tasty gear (I reckon that his mum buys it for him) and he never seems to wear the same thing twice. I suppose some girls might find him good-looking, but then they obviously need their eyes tested!

I remembered how, about three months ago, as I was walking to school and was nearly at the gates, Beacon ran past me and threw bright pink dye all over me. I screamed. I felt like killing him. My jacket was ruined, it was all in my hair, it was terrible, and he just ran past laughing. Now you see what I mean – psychopath. But what was worse, when I told my mum, she asked what I had done to make him throw the dye over me. I had to beg her to believe that I hadn't done a thing to him! Then Mum came up to the school and we, as well as Beacon, had to see the headmaster and in front of everyone Beacon denied it! I couldn't believe it, the bare-faced liar. The thing is, his face was the picture of an angel and they believed him. I hate him. No wonder his parents split up. With him living under their roof causing havoc, it must've been hard for them to live together in peace! The thought of him made me angry, and my feelings of self-pity soon disappeared.

'Kiesha, do you think Grandfather's gone to heaven?' asked Patrice.

''Course he has, stupid, he was a good bloke.'

'I hope so. I think I might start going back to Children's Church to make sure.'

'How is going back to Children's Church gonna tell you if Grandfather's gone to heaven? You have just got to believe and wait until you get there to find out. On the other hand, I'm not so sure if you will be going there,' I laughed.

Patrice looked me dead in the eye. 'You're so wicked, you are, you never have a kind word to say about anybody. You tell lies. No wonder Aunt Helen and Uncle Lyndon separated, it must've been terrible having you as a child,' she blurted out.

Then she leapt out of her chair and stormed out of the room, banging the door behind her. I couldn't speak. How could she say something like that? I felt my insides plunge to an all-time low. It was nothing to do with me that my parents couldn't get on. That's what everyone must think of me, I thought to myself. It's funny how things come round in a full circle. The awful thing was that I had thought about that possibility before: not that I was so terrible my parents couldn't live together, but that my being there was perhaps not helping the situation between them, and that it just might have been easier if I wasn't around.

I sat staring out of the window.

I heard Aunt Audrey call out goodbye and the front door slam. Thank God, I thought, I'm glad they've gone. Mum popped her head around the door.

'All right, chicken?' she asked.

I nodded. She always calls me that when she's in a good mood, so I didn't look at her but kept staring out of the window. I was afraid I might let out something that I wanted to keep to myself.

'We're going home soon, so get yourself ready.' She smiled and was gone.

I got up slowly from the window ledge, turning the thoughts over in my mind. Hmm, I wonder what was the *real* reason for Mum and Dad splitting up. I knew that they had argued sometimes, but I couldn't see why a few arguments should lead to a separation. I don't know, would I ever find out why?

TWO

I slammed the front door shut behind me and half walked, half ran towards the bus stop, but as I turned the corner the bus was just pulling into the stop. I put my head down, clutched my bag tightly under my arm and ran like a maniac. The driver kept the door open for me and as I neared the bus I could hear people booing: 'Ferell, booo, get off, get off the bus you stupid cow.'

I knew who they were, it was like this whenever I caught the bus at this time. I climbed the stairs and found the top packed with school kids in green uniforms, everyone looking identical. It was bottle green and you had to wear a white shirt with it; even the girls had to wear

13

a tie. Most of the boys were sitting at the back of the bus and the girls in the middle or at the very front. It seemed as though the whole school was there. I recognised most faces. There were graffiti everywhere: 'Water Lane Possee Rule', 'Kim loves Pete' and stuff like that. Smoke was coming from the back: some of those boys think they're right tough and smoke to prove it. I just think they are stupid. I looked for a spare seat and spied one near the back, next to an old man. As I walked towards it and sat down I thought, he's chancing it a bit, getting on the bus at this time in the morning.

There was so much noise I didn't hear it at first, but he didn't need a microphone, his mouth was so big. 'Oi, Ferell, who had their hand up your skirt last night, eh?' shouted out Delaney Rowbottom.

I turned to face him and, putting on my best voice, said, 'Well, Rowbottom, it certainly wasn't you. From my understanding of the situation, *you* have some deadly disease that not even pen–nee–cill–in,' I emphasised, 'can cure.' It turned my back on him.

'Oi, what you trying to say Ferell, eh?' he shouted, obviously none too pleased with my reply. He stood and made to come down towards me. I turned around again and said in my Lady Di voice, 'Rowbottom, are you upset? Oh dear, never mind, the truth always hurts.' And smiled.

The bus was in uproar. Everybody was in fits of laughter, which made Delaney even more mad. He stormed down to my seat, fists clenched, in a fighting mood. I was a little frightened – well, hmm, maybe a *little* bit more than frightened then! I was planning what would be the best thing to do when suddenly the old man next to me came to my rescue.

''Ere son, leave her alone. You started it, you're just getting a bit of your own medicine back, go on.'

Delaney stood over me, fuming. 'Yeah, but she shamed

14

me, man. In front of everyone.'

'So what, ain't that the same thing you did to her?'

Delaney looked down at me and pointed his finger. 'You wait Ferell, you're for it,' and stormed off to the back of the bus. I turned and thanked the old man, who told me not to worry. I told him that I wasn't.

He said, 'All you have to do to a bully is confront him and then he has to back down.' I smiled and thought, my knight in shining armour!

The way they push and shove to get each other off the bus, you would think the kids were eager to get to school. Coming down the stairs is right tricky, the danger being that someone could push you from behind and you could end up breaking your neck. I made sure Delaney got off the bus before me, otherwise I'm sure he would have taken the opportunity to quicken *my* exit. Walking in the school gates, I saw him up ahead with his mates. He turned to look back at me and I just smiled really cool.

Climbing the stairs to the second floor for my first lesson I met Stacey Bailey, my best friend. She's not a bad-looking girl: she has buck teeth, but she has a set of orthopaedic braces – I think that's what you call them, they make your teeth look like a mass of metal in your mouth – and her hair in extension plaits as well, which make her look attractive. She's a little fatter than me, but then I don't consider myself to be fat. One thing, though, she's brainy. Whatever the teacher says, Stacey remembers. Computer brain, that's what I called her sometimes. Whenever I had any problems, I'd tell Stace – that's what I really called her – and she was always able to throw some light on to the matter or advise me in some way. A good kid. Not many of the others at school seemed to like Stace, though. It wasn't that they actually disliked her; it was more that they never seemed to notice her, perhaps because she was so quiet. I bet if they knew how bright she was, and how she could keep secrets, they would try and be friends. Stace was *my* friend and I wanted to keep her all to myself.

As we walked along the corridor I told her about what had happened on the bus. She said she didn't know why I bothered to answer Delaney, I should've just ignored him.

'But Stace, I couldn't. My name depended on it.'

'Kiesha, will you never learn? By not answering him, you would have risen above the occasion, leaving him in a ditch,' she sighed.

I thought for a while. 'Hm, maybe you're right Stace, but anyway, I'm still glad I said what I did. It serves him right.'

The biology teacher, Mr Andrews, was already in the lab. Stace and I were the last to come in.

'Well, hurry yourselves, Kiesha and Stacey. It's not holiday time or a free for all. Move.' We quickly hurried to our benches and sat on stools. I looked to my right and saw Delaney sniggering.

'Delaney, what's the joke? Please tell us as I'm sure we would enjoy it as much as you.'

Delaney straightened up. 'Nothing, sir,' he said innocently.

'Well, let's hope you've done your homework.'

My turn to snigger. He looked daggers at me.

The lesson was boring as usual: Mr Andrews droning on and on. I couldn't see how it was relevant to my career to know the growth rate of fungus. I wished he would drink a bottle of fungicide, that would shut him up. I looked at Stacey from the corner of my eye; as usual she was getting carried away with the lesson. She seemed to be shaking her head in agreement with everything Mr Andrews said and every time her head moved her plaits shook. Some fell across her face and brushed against her eyes, but her eyelashes were so long that they brushed the plaits aside. I think her profile is much better than her frontal view. Now I know why film stars have photos

16

taken from 'their best side'. Stacey wasn't as dark as me but, sad to say for her, I think she is going to have teenage spots, poor thing! Another thing about her, I told her to get some Vaseline lip balm, because she suffers from cracked lips, but I told her that she'd probably grow out of it. She seemed right involved with the lesson, her eyes held a dreamy, faraway look. I wondered if she fancied old Andrews. But then I thought, no, never. I looked at her again and then at Andrews. I'm sure he was about sixty, I think he was married. Oh, well, different strokes for different folks. His hair, what was left of it, hadn't been combed for ages. Perhaps he was becoming a Rasta, I laughed to myself. He had on a dirty old jacket that looked as if it had never seen the inside of a dry-cleaner's. What a mess.

I put my elbows on the table and my hand under my chin and wondered what a bright, good-looking girl – certainly not ugly – was doing in a place like this. When I leave school, I might go to college. I want to run my own business, so I suppose I'll probably end up at some college. I don't know what sort of business, but one thing I do know for sure: I'll be boss.

Yeah, running my own business. Employing people to fetch and carry for me. I could imagine it all: sitting in *my* office, talking to clients on *my* private telephone line, making big deals that involved millions and could be clinched only on *my* final word. Giving orders to *my* personal assistant, who would pass them on to *my* secretary, and they would both be at *my* beck and call. Sitting in *my* office with its plush thick shag-pile carpets. And leading off the office – in case I had to stay overnight – there'd be a bedroom, all pink with a double bed and a duck-down quilt, just like the one that Mum has.

'Miss Kiesha Tashana Ferell, *madam* so-and-so is waiting outside to see you,' says my efficient secretary.

'Oh, tell them to wait a moment while I tie up this deal.' I wave my hand to her and she walks backwards, bowing to me, out of the door. I then finish off filing my nails to perfection, like Dominique Devereux in *Dynasty*. Going to work in nothing but designer clothes, perhaps even dresses and suits designed exclusively for me. A few diamond clusters adorn my fingers, not too many, otherwise it would appear that I had no taste. I glance up and look at my fox-fur coat hanging on its specially made coat-hanger over in the far corner of the office.

'Oh, the price of success,' I think to myself.

I check myself in the mirror and I like what I see, no smudges or streaks to lower my self-made standards. I finger my curls with a manicured nail, perfect, perfect! I breathe out scented breath and, delicately placing my hand on my chest, I pout my lips and lean across to buzz *my* secretary . . .

'Kiesha, Kiesha, *Kiesha Ferell*, see me after school,' shouted Mr Andrews. The class was laughing. Mr Andrews was red in the face. Oh, no, I must have been daydreaming again, I thought.

Stacey looked at me, shaking her head. Then she shrugged. What am I going to tell Mum? She usually gets in just after me and if I'm late again she'll go mad. I know that when old Andrews keeps you in, he goes on and on, virtually repeating the entire lesson, and expecting you to ask him questions, as if you're really interested. *And* he gives you additional homework to do! What a drag.

I walked out of the double glass doors of the school building feeling depressed. I was trying to find an excuse for being late. If I told Mum that Mr Andrews was picking on me, she would come up to the school and give him a piece of her mind. I tried to think of something else that would get her feeling sympathetic towards me – nothing. Then I tried to steel myself for the onslaught. I was halfway across the playground when I heard someone shouting:

'Hey, babe, kick the ball?'

I carried on walking.

'Oi, darling.'

I looked. I froze. It was Jamal Hinds. *Jamal Hinds.* My mouth dropped open like a fish. I couldn't believe it.

'Yeah, you, sweetheart,' he smiled.

I pointed to myself. By now he was only a yard or so away.

'Not to worry, I'm nearly there now.' He bent and picked up the ball, which had rolled itself back towards him. He put his hand on my shoulder and said 'You all right?' He was obviously concerned about me, I thought, and wondered why.

'Yes,' I whispered, though it was an effort to get it out. I thought I might collapse under the weight of his hand on my shoulder. Then he winked at me and walked back to his game of football with the ball under his arm.

I took a deep breath and slowly walked towards the gate, a bit unsteady, trying my hardest not to look back. I thought I would wait until I was on the other side, then I would look. I considered what had just taken place. *Jamal Hinds!* I'm sure there wasn't one night in which I didn't dream about him. He is so gorgeous, I could've eaten him for breakfast, dinner, and tea. Wow! I walked slowly along the fence watching the boys playing football and spied him among the other boys. He stood out a mile from them. He must be a least six foot tall. He had on tight red shorts. His legs start off on the ground and finish somewhere near his shoulders. He's an Ovaltiny colour with a big blob of condensed milk mixed in and his body looks as though it has been chiselled by an expert craftsman, his biceps and triceps made of granite. I could just imagine the adrenalin pumping through his veins as he ran after the ball! His pectoral muscles were straining

19

against his shirt, threatening to tear it. He is built like The Hulk! I stopped and peered through the railings to get a good look. It was a good thing I was holding on to the bars, because Jamal saw me and waved. I nearly slid to the ground and had to keep taking deep breaths – was this really happening? I felt like screaming, but managed to walk casually to the bus stop.

I stood in a daze. I don't remember when the bus arrived or how I got on it, didn't even know that I was sitting on it until Liza Shaw, who lives up the road from me (she must've been coming home from work), tapped me on the shoulder and asked me if I was getting off. I was right out of it.

And when I got home Mum was livid.

'What time do you call this, young lady? What with young kids getting abducted by perverted men, you just stroll in here, like you've come of age. Now where have you been?'

I told her what had happened; that I had been kept in school by Mr Andrews for daydreaming during his lessons. I couldn't tell her about Jamal, she would go wild and want to come up to the school. Jamal – just thinking about him helped me to bear the brunt of Mum's temper.

Three

It was the next day. I put my key in the lock and let myself in to Mama Tiny's house. I stood in the passage and shivered. A coldness came over me. I wonder if Mama Tiny has left the back door open, I thought.

'Mama Tiny, Mama Tiny,' I shouted. No answer. Oh

well, she must be out. I walked past Grandfather's study and thought I heard a noise. I stopped. Oh my goodness, burglars. I wanted to run but found that my knees were about to give way. I tried to scream but my jaws locked tight. I wondered if this was what it was like to be strangled – no sound could come out of my mouth. Somehow I managed to push open the door and step into the study and my eyes nearly fell out of my head when I saw Mama Tiny's face. Her small bright eyes were red and puffy, her usually radiant bronze-coloured skin had lost its glow, even her chubby cheeks had sunk and her little button nose with the hump at the tip was running.

'Mama Tiny, what have they done to you? Do you remember what they looked like? Oh no, what shall I do? Shall I call the police?' I shrieked.

Mama Tiny looked so small sitting in the worn leather armchair that had been Grandfather's. Tears spilled from her eyes and ran down her face.

'Hosea, Hosea, mi miss yu, why did yu ave fi leave mi ee? Yu said dat we would always be togedda, but yu bruck yur promise an gawn weh,'she cried softly. She leaned across the desk and put her head in her small but strong hands. Those hands, I thought to myself, have nursed, fed and comforted her children and their children, and loved Grandfather. Her face was completely wet. She was unaware that I was in the room with her. The way she was crying she looked as though she was in a lot of pain.

'Hosea, mi gwine wait right here till mi die,' said Mama Tiny, looking exhausted her grief was so heavy, and she just slumped in the armchair, eyes closed, mind blank, waiting, waiting . . .

'Mama Tiny, what have they done to you? Do you remember what they looked like?' I shrieked again.

Slowly, she opened her eyes. A moan escaped from her lips. I couldn't help it: I just flung myself down at her feet, hugging her knees and crying 'Mama Tiny, Mama Tiny, what have they done to my nan?' She began to stroke my hair, whimpering 'Hosea, Hosea.' Next thing, I was crying too. The room gradually grew silent and still. Mama Tiny began to sing:

> By the rivers of Babylon
> Where we sat down
> Yea we wept
> When we remembered Zion . . .

She hummed the tune quietly.

'Mama Tiny, how many were there?'

She seemed not to hear me. I sat up and gently stroked her arm. 'Can't you remember?'

Mama Tiny stirred in her chair. 'What yu say chile?' she sniffed.

'I said, how many men attacked you?'

Mama Tiny blew her nose. 'What yu talkin bout chile?'

I got to my knees, pushing my face closer to hers, and very slowly, saying each word clearly, I repeated, 'How many burglars attacked you?' Mama Tiny frowned. She wiped her face and sat up straight in the chair.

'Kiesha, what yu seying ee, what burglar, yu mean tief?'

I wondered for a moment if Mama Tiny had been hit over the head and had lost her memory. 'Mama Tiny' – I spoke slowly so that I wouldn't confuse her any more than she already was – 'you've been burgled.'

'Whaat!' she shouted. She jumped up, nearly knocking me over, and grabbing the statue of the Eiffel Tower which Grandfather had brought back after a coach trip to Paris, she dashed out of the door, with me hot on her heels.

'Where dem dere?' she bawled out in anger, waving the Eiffel Tower in the air. I held on to her jumper for dear life.

Mama Tiny charged up the stairs, taking two steps at a

time. Who would have believed that less than two minutes ago she didn't look as though she had enough strength to pick up a pin!

We stood in her bedroom looking around for what had been taken – nothing. We went into all the bedrooms, even the bathroom – nothing. Mama Tiny marched back into her bedroom. She sat on her bed, I stood in front of her. 'Kiesha.'

'Yes, Mama Tiny.'

'Who tell yu seh me did ave tief bruck mi house?'

'Well, hmm, no one,' I whispered. The truth began to dawn on me.

'Sooo, how yu know?' said Mama Tiny, putting her hands on her hips.

'Well, I saw you crying and it looked as though someone had hit you over the head, so I thought that it could only be burglars, because no one else could ever beat you up and expect to get away with it!'

Mama Tiny's eyes became moist. She beckoned me to come to her. I went over to the bed and sat down next to her. She put her arm around me and squeezed.

'Kiesha, me love mi lickle grandpicknee, because I know she love me.' She kissed me.

I felt like crying, I wasn't sure why, but all the same I could feel tears on the way.

'Yes, I love you,' was all I could say.

'Chile, yu right, it was a tief fi true dat did tek weh yu Grandfadda from mi, an all like now, is when mi need im.' She heaved and tightened her grip on me.

'Oh, Mama Tiny,' I cried. 'You were crying for Grandfather,' and the tears fell. It seemed like an hour that Mama Tiny and I sat with our arms around each other.

I pulled out the tissue that I kept up my sleeve and blew my nose. Mama Tiny kissed the top of my head. 'Well chile, let's gawn inna de kitchen an start cook we food ee.' I followed her out of the door and she showed me for the

23

umpteenth time how to peel the green bananas.

'Now yu split it part weh an peel off de skin wid yur hand, like dis,' she demonstrated patiently for me.

'Mama Tiny, I'll never get it right. Look at my hands, are you sure they won't stain?'

'Kiesha, yu give up too easy. Yu ave fi learn how to peel banana, or next ting yu husband leave yu. Yu know dem seh dat how fi ketch a man is tru him belly,' she laughed.

'Well, I'm not getting married, unless he's like Grandfather.'

'Oh chile, wait till yu turn ooman, is den yu gwine talk differently.'

I was just about to answer her when I thought of Jamal. Hmm, I thought to myself, I wonder if he likes green bananas.

'Show me how to peel them again, please, Mama Tiny.'

The evening was still light. Inside the kitchen it was very humid. Even the ceiling was sweating! Mama Tiny had opened the window and the back door to let in some air. The wallpaper with strings of onions and tomatoes and potatoes on it was peeling from the top in the corner. No wonder, the steam must have done that over the years. The windows with their red and white nets and fancy pot plants were all steamed up too: mind you, the plants thrived. The shelves above the deep-freeze were a mass of bottles and jars, some with labels, some without. I couldn't work out how Mama Tiny knew what was in the ones without labels; the only one I knew was the large tub of Season-All, but only because Mum had an identical one at home. In the corner, near the back door, was a mop and bucket. Mama Tiny always kept it there in the daytime, and put it outside at night. Whenever water got on the floor, out would come the mop and the water would disappear. Dad used to take the mickey out of Mama Tiny, doing an impersonation of her with her mop.

'Mine yurself everbady, mine yu foot slip and yu drop,'

24

he'd say, pretending to mop the floor.

'Lyndon, move yurself an come out mi weh. Yu too trublesome,' Mama Tiny would say, kissing her teeth. It was funny.

'Set up de table, Kiesha,' asked Mama Tiny.

I took out the small drop-leaf table which lived between the sink and the deep-freeze, pulled out one side and began to set the table. Aunt Audrey had bought Mama Tiny the dinner set one Christmas, boasting about how expensive it was. Well, I reckon that she was conned: it was horrible. The pots on the stove with the bananas and dumplings in were bubbling away and the fish in the duchie pot was simmering. Everything smelled good, but it was stifling! Mama Tiny dished the food into serving bowls – you know, even if Mama Tiny was eating by herself, she would still set the table as though she had guests. We sat and Mama Tiny said grace, and she said 'Amen' I echoed her. Mama Tiny began to demolish the food, and gradually the pattern on her plate emerged. You could hear her dentures clacking against each other – she knew they were too loose in her mouth, but they were comfortable!

'You can tell the bananas I peeled,' I grinned.

'Nar worry, practice mek perfect,' she said.

'Mum doesn't cook West Indian food a lot, she says that it takes too much time, but when we lived with Dad, she cooked it every day and I was wondering . . .' I said, as an idea began to formulate in my brain. 'Perhaps if you lived with us at least we would have it most of the time.' I waited, holding my breath.

'Yur mudda put yu up to dis ee?' she said, not taking her eyes off the plate.

'Hmm, not really.'

In actual fact they had all had a family conference at Aunt Audrey's stately home in the suburbs. By 'they' I

25

mean Mum and Uncle Tim and his wife and Uncle Robert-o, *not* us kids. The conclusion was that Mama Tiny would be better off living with one of her children and that one was *Mum*! Aunt Audrey, with her newly done hairdo, long red nails and *full* make-up, had sat on her backside, giving 101 excuses as to why she 'couldn't possibly have Mama Tiny living with her'. It might lower the tone of the neighbourhood, she said, though not in so many words. I don't know why she was making all that fuss about Ilford; I'm sure if you looked you would find a ghetto or two there too! Big deal. Mum exploded at Aunt Audrey and Uncle Tim started to shout at her in *Jamaican*, making Aunt Audrey jump out of her seat and rush to close the windows so that the neighbours couldn't hear his voice, which made Uncle Tim even more vexed. The muscles in his neck stood out and his eyes bulged. Then his wife, Auntie Susie, got up and tried to put her arms around him to calm him down, which made him worse.

Renita and Patrice were sitting on the piano stool, heads bent, trying to look invisible, and I knew that they were embarrassed by their mother's behaviour. I was glad that Uncle Stanley wasn't present; nobody could control him. He was like a thunderstorm, a major earthquake and nuclear fallout all rolled into one. He was six foot two and half inches. His arms started at the top of his head and finished at his knees, his legs started somewhere buried under the ground and ended at his armpits. His voice was really deep: you could hear it rumbling from his knees and when it came out of his mouth, it was damaging to the eardrums!

Ever since I can remember, he has never got on with Aunt Audrey (and he isn't the only one). 'Dat ooman she nar mi sister, she is no relation to mi, she is an embarrrassment to the black race, especially to black ooman. And as fi her man, im,' he huffed, 'im need a good kick inna im pants, an it just might shake up im brain.'

You can see what I mean: Uncle Stanley doesn't mince his words!

Anyway, he was in Jamaica on business and visiting Auntie Thelma, who lived there and who was the eldest child. I think everyone felt secretly that Jamaica was probably the best place for him then, because he gets really angry with Aunt Audrey when 'she a pappyshow' and because he gets on well with Mama Tiny (I think he's her favourite). The thought of *them* discussing what to do with *her*, like she was a family pet, would have made him blow his top! Throughout this so-called 'meeting', Uncle Robin – oops, sorry, Roberto – never said a word. Whenever he looked as though he might get up to say something, Aunt Audrey waved her hand (she thought she was the Queen sometimes) and he shut up and sat down. Or he would open his mouth and someone else who had a stronger point or voice would get in before him, and he would be left like a fish out of water, opening and shutting it. It was quite funny.

Well, five hours later, and after a heavy silence, Mum said that if she could talk Mama Tiny round she would like her to come and live with us.

You know, I sometimes wonder about adults. They complain about us kids – especially teenagers – *we* are supposed to be going through a 'difficult stage'. I think the official term is 'identity crisis' but after that meeting I felt they had all been childish themselves. Five hours of near bloodshed to settle what was going to happen to their mother, whom they all said they loved. Then, in the space of a minute or so, it was all solved.

If that's what it is to be an adult, well, thanks but no thanks, I'd rather be a teenager.

Anyway, back to the green bananas and fish.

'Hmm, Mama Tiny, I would really like you to come and

live with us. Not only would it be good for us, but it could be good for you too. I mean, look at today when I thought that you had been attacked in your own home and burgled. Well, living alone, anything could happen to you and it could be days before anyone found out!'

Mama Tiny picked a fish bone out of her mouth and wiped her fingers on a napkin.

'Chile, if I leave dis house, who will keep de memory of Grandfadda alive ee? Anyway, I cyaan dash weh all me tings dem, yur house cyaan hold dem. An again, look how far mi would ave fi come fi go a church, an de market is so near here, I can walk. I cyaan find no reason fi leave.' She dished up some more fish.

We ate in silence for a while. I tried to rack my brains for a good reason for Mama Tiny to come and live with us, every now and again sneaking a look at her as she ate. Suddenly it hit me.

'Mama Tiny, I have a really good reason for you to come and live with us.' I paused for her to react to what I'd said. She looked up and waited for me to continue.

'Well, Mama Tiny, Mum and I love you. We love your company. We love your sense of humour. We love your cooking. We love you singing gospel songs around the house.' (Actually Mum said she didn't mind Mama Tiny singing; what drove her mad was being badgered about not going to church and living a godly life.) 'In fact we just love everything about you,' I said all in one breath.

'Well, dere's nuttin I can say to dat. Okay, I ave fi tink bout it.'

I was a little hurt because what I had said was true and I mean, it's not every day that you tell someone you love them and why; I at least expected a kiss or something. So I changed the subject by talking about the new shoes Mum had bought me. Mama Tiny didn't seem too interested and I could see she was tired, so I said I'd go home. I never mentioned another word to Mama Tiny about living with us until she actually came.

28

I loved my bedroom; but right now it made me feel a bit funny inside. On one side of my heart I really, really loved Mama Tiny – but on the other side I loved this room too. I couldn't cut it in half, could I? I'd just have to get used to living in that small box room somehow. But meanwhile, I decided, I was going to enjoy my room while I could.

Mum had let me choose my own decorations. I had wanted peach and black as the colour scheme but she said that black was morbid, so either I had to have peach and white or she would decorate it the way she wanted to and I would have to put up with it. I quite liked the peach embossed walls and the white Artexed ceiling. Even the bed linen was peach and white. I secretly thought that peach and black would really have been too much, but there was no way that I was going to tell Mum she was right, that would be fatal. My mum's deadly like that: if she predicts something and it happens and you might've been wrong, she continually rams it down your throat until you choke on it because you're sick and tired of eating it!

On the wall I had stuck ten snazzy mirror tiles. The tiles were so telltale, nothing escaped their attention! In the sales I had bought a woollen 'tube' skirt in black to go with a peach padded-shouldered sweatshirt and peach shoes. Well, I'm of slim stature and unfortunately my Forever (that's what I call the dreaded monthly) had been due or thereabout (*it* did its own thing – turned up when *it* felt like it, just like boys and bad news), and my stomach looked as if I had stuffed a football up there! It was really awful.

My dad had bought me a *brilliant* stereo. It's one of those small ones with a turntable and radio and re-a-lly powerful speakers. I love music. Prince is ace (peach and black), Terence Trent D'Arby, those plaits in his hair – ooooooohhhh – and those eyes with sweeping long lashes . . . But the man of my dreams is MICHAEL JACKSON.

When he sings 'Billie Jean' (which I've worn out because I play it every day), he sings it for me and when he makes those 'ooh, ooh' sounds at the back of his throat I know he's choked up 'cos he's got me on his mind. My friends think I'm crazy; they say that Michael's mad, because he treats those animals of his like human beings. 'Yeah,' I say, 'only because animals are sometimes preferable to some human beings!' They can't say anything to that. He seems so gentle and kind, he just needs someone to love him (me), who can understand him (me), someone he can dance with who's as good as him (me), someone to get on with his sister, Janet (me) – and someone he can spend his money on (me).

I had his pictures all over one wall and no matter where I was in my room his eyes would follow me everywhere, unblinking, mesmerised, caught up in wonderment. Oohh!

I stretched out on my back across the bed; the air in the room seemed so light. I breathed in deeply, drinking in the quietness, drinking in the soft light streaming through the window, drinking in the potpourri fresh-air sachet hanging from the curtail rail and it came to me again that when Mama Tiny moved in with us, she would have my room. She had so much stuff that the other bedroom would be too small. My heart sank inside me once more. *Would* I be able to give it up? I felt sad. I had been the one to tell Mama Tiny that she was welcome to come here at any time and we would welcome her into our house with open arms, but now I was secretly hoping she would delay so that I could have my room a bit longer. I opened the wardrobes, took out the new shoes Mum had bought me and put them on. They were a little tight and I was trying to stretch them. I walked over to the stereo and put on my *BAD* LP:

Hey pretty baby with the high heels on
You give me fever
Like I've never, ever known
You're just a product of loveliness . . .

I stood in front of the mirror, wrapped my arms tightly around my shoulders and waist and danced to the song. I leaned my head on my shoulder and half closed my eyes. 'Michael, Michael,' I cooed. I slowly raised my head and immediately our eyes met. It was like plugging in the electric curling tongs – a huge zap of electricity charged out from both of us, threatening to overtake us, sending us out from the earth into space, among the stars, flowing through the galaxy:

. . . Just hold me baby I'm in ecstasy . . .

I threw my arms around my head, still dancing to the music.

. . . The way you make me feel . . .

He knew my heart. He sang words that were for me.

'Kiesha, Kiesha, turn that music down. What are you doing up there, having a disco?'
   I leapt across the room to the stereo and turned it down. My nerves were like jelly. Mum's voice was *so* loud, like a sharp knife cutting right through your brain. She always seems to cut in between me and Michael. I admit we do talk a lot to each other, well, not out loud, but sort of spiritually. I don't mean spiritually spooky, like 'Are you with us, Uncle Albert?' – no way – but, you know, in a way that doesn't need physical words, just a lot of eye contact and imagination.
   Once Mum caught me talking to Michael. I don't know

31

how long she'd been standing there, but she must've heard and seen quite a bit because I heard her on the phone to Aunt Susie later telling her that I had been talking and staring at 'pictures on the wall'! She made it sound as if I was a lunatic or something, and I don't know what Aunt Susie told her but Mum said she wasn't having any more (any more of what, I don't know) and that she would buy me a dog to keep me company! Well, she didn't and anyway, I don't want a dog.

I wish my dad was home. We used to have a great time together, I could tell him anything. He understood about Michael, although I didn't go into depth about our relationship, but I'm sure he would've understood. I think!

Anyway, I'd better see that Mum wants. I wonder if she misses Dad?

Four

Monday mornings were so depressing. Even the thought of the summer holidays coming couldn't liven me up or make me a little more interested in Miss Pettigrew's English class. I had been lucky to get the desk by the window and I spent most of the time looking out — freedom. Her voice was like a bee, buzzzz, buzzzzzz. I felt like rolling up my exercise book and taking a swat at her. I sat there in the stuffy classroom, just staring at Miss Pettigrew. She was quite plump and sort of cuddly. She had been at this school for years. Brent Collins said that his mum had had her for her English teacher too! She seemed concerned about us and sometimes asked questions about how we were getting on: was school all right, was home life fine? I wasn't sure whether it was *real* concern or whether she was just being nosy. I didn't like to tell her anything, or anyone else for that matter.

She rarely kept you back from school if you misbehaved; usually she just spoke to you and told you to be good and off you went. She was my form teacher.

'Now, Class 2E, before we start this morning we have a new addition to the class. I want you to treat her g-e-n-t-l-y and help her around the school as much as possible. Now . . .' The door opened and in walked Mrs Harper, the deputy head, with a black woman and a girl. The girl was nearly as tall as the woman and had her hair in two plaits that sat on her shoulders. She looked a bit Indianish, especially with her hair parted down the centre. She was skinny and looked as if she needed some of Mama Tiny's cooking to fatten her up. She had a sort of bored look on her face, as though she wasn't bothered whether she was joining this class or not. The woman looked more interesting; you could see that they were mother and daughter but the mother was plump. Perhaps she ate all the girl's dinner: I wanted to laugh.

'Class 2E,' said Mrs Harper, 'this is Janeese Sharack. Say hello.' She smiled and I thought she should have been on *Play School*. 'Hello,' we all boomed in unison, and Janeese smiled for a split second and said 'hello' back. The black woman just smiled.

'Oh thank you, Mrs Harper,' buzzed Miss Pettigrew. 'Welcome, Janeese.' She turned to Mrs Sharack. 'She will be fine now. You may come for her at 3.45 p.m. if you wish,' she dismissed her. Mrs Harper was already out of the door. 'Now, where can I put you to sit? Hmm.' She looked around the classroom. 'Ah, let me see, er Stacey Bailey, would you move your things to the empty desk beside Gail Bacon and you, Janeese, can sit next to Kiesha Ferell. Kiesha please make Janeese very welcome.'

I was paralysed with shock. How could Miss Pettigrew

33

move Stacey, the brains of this two-girl outfit? She knew we were best friends. Who was going to help me with my class work? Who was going to prod me at the right time and provide me with the right answer when I was asked a question in the middle of a daydream? Could this Janeese Sharwhatever-her-name-is fit the bill? I was fuming. I smiled a tight smile as she sat down. Well, no one was going to force me to be friends with her. How could you be friends with someone you hardly knew? Miss Pettigrew must think that we're animals or something. A stray creature comes into a fold and we just nuzzle up to one another, and 'That's all right mate, you're in with us now.'

The more I thought about it the more angry I became. I folded my arms and sat there scowling, eyebrows knitted together, lips pursed, shoulders hunched over. I was plotting how I could wangle getting Stacey back to sit with me. I looked around at Stacey and saw she was engrossed in what Miss Pettigrew was saying as usual. That made it worse: didn't Stacey miss me? Was she pleased that she had been moved? I'd have thought that being away from me would've made her unable to study during the lessons, but obviously not. Didn't I mean anything to her? I gazed out of the window and let my mind drift, ending up on a desert island, after the plane that was flying me to Brazil for an exotic holiday had crashed. I had managed to swim ashore, where I fell asleep. When I woke up, the sun was blindingly hot and I had to shield my eyes with my hands. My clothes were in shreds on my body, but you couldn't see anything! My plaits were wet, the water drops were like jewels in my hair and I looked like the girl on telly (advertising cigars, I think), rising out of the sea.

I stood up and dusted the sand from my legs and what was left of my clothes. In that hot climate, the sand bleached white by the sun, the warm water beckoning me, a row of palm trees behind me, a place anyone would describe as paradise, I felt alone. Who could I call on for help? I turned around – nothing, no one. Then I realised that I had been marooned on a desert island. Now some people might enjoy that, but as far as I was concerned, it was bad luck. It wouldn't have been too bad if someone else had been marooned with me but . . . No, wait, there was someone coming through the palm trees, walking towards me with a basket in her hand. No, it can't be, but yes, it's Janeese. What's she doing here? She walked up to me, knelt in front of me and took the cover off her basket. In it was a coconut already cut open for me to drink from, some cooked fish wrapped in banana leaves and some mangoes and sugar cane for us to share. I smiled at her and she held out the coconut for me to drink . . .

'Hello, hello,' Janeese prodded me.

'Oh, thank you, you're so kind,' I beamed at her, holding out my hand to take the coconut. She pointed at the teacher.

'Kiesha Ferell, what did you think of that line?' buzzed a voice in front of me, zooming me back to reality.

'Pardon, Miss Pettigrew?' I gulped deeply, stalling for time, trying to work out what she was on about.

'I said, for the tenth time for your benefit, what did that line conjure up for you, Kiesha?' Her lips pursed into a thin line.

'Well, I, hmm, I'm not quite sure, it, hmm, it, hmm, didn't really do much, Miss. Perhaps I need to hear it again, only this time slower. Do you think I can?' I put my hand on my chest to steady my nerves and smiled sweetly. It was difficult. My heart was beating fifteen to the dozen, my face felt as though it was going to crack from the effort of smiling and my brain was on strike, refusing to dig deep into my vast imagination that seemed to have dried up! I gulped again: maybe a huge dose of oxygen might shake up the grey matter. I gave a sidewards glance at Janeese, who was straining to prevent herself from putting her hand in the air. *She* obviously knew the answer. This was what I meant about sitting next to someone who didn't know me.

'Yes, Janeese, perhaps you have something interesting to say?'

'Well, Miss, that particular line "The heat within stopped the time of day" made me think of the time I was on holiday in Trinidad and I was sitting in my auntie's house and she didn't have air conditioning and it was so hot even to lift your hand was such an effort and we just sat there like statues and it was as though time had really stopped,' Janeese said breathlessly.

'Oh, my dear, what a vivid explanation! Well done,' Miss Pettigrew beamed. 'As for Kiesha Ferell, who I'm sure wasn't paying her fullest attention, I would like to see *her* after school. Now then, for homework . . .'

'That horrible show-off girl,' I fumed. She tried to show me up in front of everybody. It was a good thing that it was old Pettigrew. What if it had been anyone else? I would definitely have been in for it. That was that – I didn't want to sit next to her again.

The bell rang and in less than two minutes the classroom was empty. You wouldn't have believed that there had been nearly thirty children in here. I sat looking like Little Bo Peep, hoping that she wouldn't go on and on.

'Now dear, I've been meaning to talk to you for some time now. A few of your other teachers have commented on the fact that during their classes you seem to be preoccupied, staring into space. I myself have noticed this and I was wondering if there was something wrong. Are you finding the class work too much? You aren't being bullied or anything like that? Now, you can tell me. What about your home life, hmm? I know that your parents have separated, is that the problem?'

I felt really weird when she said that. I mean, I can talk

about what happened to my parents to most people, even talking to my parents about it I'm okay, but the minute someone else starts on about it, it makes me want to cry. I try so hard not to, because I hate crying in front of other people. I get so embarrassed, it's like they can see right through me and I feel naked, it's horrible. So when Miss Pettigrew, with her 'concerned voice', started talking about 'how hard it must be for you being the only child, no one to turn to, feeling inadequate, what a trying time it must be,' and putting her arms around me, I felt like heaving. She patted my head; my nose ran. I felt uncomfortable, but I couldn't tell her to push off. I don't know how long we sat there, but it was really on the tip of my tongue to tell her to get lost. There she was, squashing me with her arms, reeking of lavender water, which made me want to puke, thinking she was consoling me, when in fact she was the cause of my upset. Oh, what a life! There was no alternative but to try and stop crying, calm down, smile and *get out*!

Walking to the bus stop I felt as though a cloud had purposely sought me out and settled over my head. Why is it that when people (by this I mean *adults*) think they are doing you good, in fact they make you feel ten times worse? I hadn't felt like this in ages. I remembered the last time, it was when Mum had had a go at me. I'm sure it was because of Dad's 'friend' being in his car when he came to pick me up one Saturday.

It was so stupid, but nevertheless it happened. Dad usually beeped the horn, then I would look out of the front room window, wave, shout upstairs to Mum that I was going, and out I went. This particular day, when I got to Dad's red and black convertible Jag XJS, I was surprised to find a youngish woman sitting in the front. As the car had only two doors she climbed out to let me in. I sat in the back. Dad explained that she was Marlene, a friend of his, and straight away I was on my guard. I thought something was a bit suss. Now don't get me wrong. I'm not saying that my dad can't have female friends, but this Marlene, Dad went on to explain, was a *miss* and had just fallen out with her boyfriend! As she's an old friend of Dad's, she popped in to see him. You see, I suppose you could say that my dad is nearly an eligible bachelor, and someone like Marlene could fancy her chances and be quite at home with him. Well, I didn't even say hello to her at first. I just sat looking straight ahead, but Dad asked me if I didn't have any manners, so I just about managed a 'Hello'. I had learnt from previous experience that action speaks louder than words! Anyway, Dad dropped her off at the station and we had a lovely day together. He had to pop into his office (he's a computer programmer) and showed me off to the few people there – 'Oh, isn't she sweet?' and 'Lyndon, she looks just like you.' Dad was grinning from ear to ear and I must admit I did quite enjoy the praise. I smiled like a plastic dolly, loving it.

We stopped briefly at Dad's flat to see if the postman had been and ended up as usual having a posh meal at Dad's favourite Cantonese restaurant, where all the waiters know him and fussed over us. I just *love* crab in black bean soup.

Afterwards Dad dropped me at our front door and waited as usual until I went inside before he drove off. On this particular day, once I got inside, Mum started to question me as soon as I sat down at the kitchen table.

'Did you have a nice time? Where did you go? What did you do? What did your dad buy you?'

Then she went on about Dad 'wasting his money on senseless things, I can see he hasn't changed one bit'.

When I told her that he took me to his office, she said he was showing off as usual and added, 'If only they knew what he was really like.'

She asked if he had made any additions to his flat and I

knew then that something was up! Mum always asks questions in sequence. The 'addition to the flat' was a warning signal: something was definitely brewing.

'What do you mean?' I asked.

'Oh, you know the sort of thing I mean, has he got new curtains up? Has he learnt to put away his clothes tidily? You know, your dad is so untidy,' she said, her back to me, watering the plants on the window ledge over the sink. A funny time to be watering, I thought. At 9 p.m.

As soon as she asked about new curtains and Dad getting tidier, I knew what she was getting at. She suspected what I first suspected – *Marlene*.

'Did you end up at Mr Poon's resturant?' she said, filling the kettle. 'Milo, love?'

'Yes Mum. And I'd love a cup of Milo.'

'I suppose you don't want anything to eat, you must be full,' she said.

'Yes. Do you like the new shoes Dad bought?' I showed her the box.

'Oh, they're nice. Put his hand in his pocket for a change, did he? Look like they cost quite a bit.'

We sat at the table sipping our drinks. I wanted Mum to ask me about Marlene and I didn't have to wait long.

'Who was your dad's passenger? Friend or foe?' she asked, looking into her cup.

'I'm not sure – could be either. I don't trust her though,' I said.

'Why not?' asked Mum.

'Well, she reckons herself, she thinks she's right nice. Anyway, I don't know what Dad is doing with her, she's not his sort.'

'Oh, you know what sort your Dad likes then?' said Mum softly.

'Yeah, he likes girls who make him feel like a man, that's what he said. And any girl who doesn't, he just gets rid of.'

'What – like me?' said Mum.

'No, don't be silly, Mum.' I was surprised that she came out with that.

'You listen to your father too much, that's your trouble.' Mum sipped her drink.

'That's what he says I do with you. "Just like your mum",' I mimicked.

'Oh really, you discuss me with your father, just like I'm one of his girls?' Mum pursed her lips.

''Course not, Mum. What's the matter?'

'What's the matter? You really want to know, eh? I've a good mind to stop you seeing your father so regularly and coming back with a mouth full of chat, that's what wrong. Every Saturday it's the same, you sound more and more like him.'

'That's what he says about you,' I whispered.

'There we go again. You both make me sick, you and him.' She banged her cup down.

We sat in silence, Mum deep in her thoughts. I wondered what she was thinking about. If she still loved Dad, and it didn't sound like it the way she had just had a go at me, perhaps seeing Marlene in the car had upset her. This was painful for everyone involved. Mind you, Dad seemed to be okay, but then again, you didn't really know for sure what he was thinking or feeling. I wondered if Mum or Dad ever considered my feelings and thought back to the time when they had told me they were going to separate for a time, and that they thought it would be best if I lived with Mum. Dad was going to live somewhere else. I would be able to see Dad whenever I wanted or we could arrange to see one another regularly if I preferred. I was shocked. It was like buying a dress, taking it home, deciding you didn't want it and taking it back to the shop to get a credit note so that you could come back to the shop whenever you liked and get something else to the same value. I remembered that day clearly. I'm sure my heart stopped for about ten minutes (I know that's not medically possible – but mine did!). Anyway, being the only child can be really difficult, and more so when your parents split. Sometimes I feel like a ping pong ball, backwards and forwards, knocking up points for the two of them, while I'm being bashed about, a bit carelessly I sometimes think.

What I couldn't understand now was why each still worried about what the other was up to. Is this a ray of hope? I would've thought that they couldn't care less about what the other was doing.

Mum leaned over and kissed me.
'Oh well, not your fault I suppose. Coming to bed now, chicken?' she smiled down at me.
'Yeah, I suppose so.' I didn't feel too good though. I was a bit low. Mum stood up and yawned; she looked tired.
'Can I sleep with you tonight, Mum?' I asked.
'Yeah, why not? Come on, you can keep my feet warm,' she laughed.
'Oh, Mum, those slave days are over. Anyway, this is supposed to be summer – your feet shouldn't be cold?'

Five

It was a few days later. I didn't like the look of the school dinner that day so I decided to have chips and a wally. I'd just got out of the school gates when Janeese seemed to appear out of nowhere and tapped me on the shoulder. 'Hi,' she grinned. To tell you the truth, (1) I

41

wanted to be alone, and (2) after the episode in Miss Pettigrew's class I had been trying to avoid her, traitor!

'Hi,' I managed to squeeze out between my teeth.

'Aren't you having lunch at school?'

'No.'

'Neither am I, it looks awful. Mind if I join you?'

I shrugged my shoulders. 'If you want to.' Now, there must be something chronically wrong with me. I had already made up my mind, and here I was agreeing that *she* could have lunch with me. Well, I wasn't going to make it comfortable for her.

'I fancy chips. Do you?' she asked.

'Yeah.'

'Oh, great. At least we'll have something in common, eating chips.' She beamed and then impulsively linked her arm through mine. I was caught off my guard: I'd never have guessed she'd do something like that!

'Hey, what do you think you're doing?' I tried to pull away from her. She stopped walking and looked at me, just like a puppy that has just been kicked.

'Kiesha, don't you like me?' she whispered.

I felt terrible. I gulped. 'Yeah, of course I do, silly, come on.' I held out my arm to her and we walked down the road, as though we had been friends for ages.

This is a strange phenomenon. You set your mind for or against a certain thing and think that nothing, absolutely nothing, will change your mind, and then somebody says or does something which seems to counteract your decision, and bang, everything has changed. Now I found myself friends with someone I had not even wanted to sit next to! We bought chips and decided to go and look in the shops. Janeese began to tell me all about herself. She had lived in South London most of her life, before her parents had decided to move to East London. She had an older brother called Neal. Her parents didn't seem to get on, from what I could gather. I didn't really want to pry, well,

42

not just yet, so I didn't ask any questions.

I made up my mind while we were walking around the shops that Janeese would be my best friend. I took back all that I had thought about her earlier. I thought about Stacey, who had been my best friend, and of all the favours that I had done her, but from the day that she had moved desks, she had changed. It was as though all that had happened between us had never taken place. She had no time for me any more. She was right in thick with that horrible Gail Bacon, who had brown hair, which she had streaked blonde. I called her Streaky Bacon now. I couldn't understand how Stacey could be friends with her. She wasn't on my intellectual level; I'm sure she didn't even know her ABC! Stacey must find it hard trying to communicate with her. And she was one of those girls who *loved* boys. I know, I've seen lots of them. They have no shame . . .

I remembered looking out of one of the windows in the corridor on the first floor at school one day, and Jamal (*my* friend) was standing with a group of his mates in the playground, when I saw that Streaky Bacon roll up her skirt to make it shorter (why I don't know, it was short enough), take her brush out of her bag and start to brush her hair – in the playground! Then she and her mate strolled over to the group of boys and said something – I couldn't hear, of course – and they all started laughing. Next, she walked up to Jamal and whispered something in his ear, and *he* laughed! She had her arm on his shoulder and you would have thought that she was made of rubber the way she was falling all over him. Mind you, he didn't push her off. Then, somehow, she nearly fell over (she did it on purpose; she should have broken her neck) and Jamal, *my* Jamal, caught her around the waist with his strong muscular arm. I hoped he realised that she was under age! Well, I couldn't stand any more, so I flew down the stairs and, would you believe it, when I got there, they had all

43

gone. I rushed to the school gates and was just in time to see them walking down the road. I felt like running after them, but the school bell rang and I had to get to my drama lesson.

So that was the sort of girl Stacey was hanging around with, a girl with no morals, as my mum would say.

When we got back to school, I decided to ask Janeese if she wanted to be my best friend. I didn't want to force it on her, but I mean to say, it was an offer she shouldn't refuse: I could pick and choose, so if she had any sense she'd say yes. Well, she did. So that was settled. Kiesha and Janeese. K and J. Yeah, it sounded really cool. I'd have to tell MJ (Michael, my pet name for him) and see what he thought.

When Janeese told me where she lived, I realised that it was within walking distance of my house. Great. It meant we could see each other after school. The more I thought about my friendship with Janeese, the more convinced I was that she had made a wise decision.

Sitting on the bus going home I really studied her. She said that her parents were from Trinidad and they were called 'Dougla', which meant they were of African and Indian parentage. Well whatever it was, she herself isn't bad-looking. She has crinkly sort of hair, jet black. I thought it was a bit old-fashioned to have it in two plaits. I'd soon change that, especially if she was going round with me. Her skin is smooth, like a pebble, and the colour of a Caramel Bar. She's really too thin, her legs are like matchsticks. She needs to fill out a bit more, like myself. I had noticed that from the day I started my periods I had to wear a bra – it's true, you can ask my mum, who, incidentally, laughed, I don't know why. My breasts felt really heavy and I knew that it was time to wear a bra, otherwise they would probably end up around my knees! Janeese said that she hadn't started her periods yet and that she was getting worried. I must admit, I said to her that if I

44

was her I would be worried too. I never told her that I'd only started about four months before – it was irrelevant, at least I had started. Also, some of the things she said were quite childish, like 'Who do you like best, your mum or you dad?' Now, what a stupid thing to ask. 'Both.' I mean, it goes without saying, but I put that down to not having started her periods. I have found out that when you start your periods you look at life differently!

I noticed that when she talked she liked to wave her right hand about. I wondered what would happen if you chopped her hand off, would she still be able to talk? I wanted to laugh, it would be so funny. Her sense of dress sounded really bad from what she said she had in her wardrobe. She said that her mum bought all her clothes. Well, if she hadn't told me that I would have thought that there was something drastically wrong with her dress sense. Firstly, the colours sounded really dull and boring, and they didn't sound like they were in fashion either – sort of babyish, you know, as though they should be worn by someone a lot younger – and what with her hair in plaits, well, she must've looked ten years younger!

I was so engrossed in my thoughts and only half listening to Janeese that I nearly missed my stop. I had to ring the bell three times, which made the driver brake a bit quick, and the conductor shouted up the stairs (that's where we were sitting) to stop messing about with the bell and to get off his bus. I stepped sedately down the stairs and reminded the conductor that the bus didn't belong to him, he was only an em-pl-oy-ee, if he cared to remember, and that the customer is always right! I had to impress upon Janeese that there was a right way to do things and that you must never, no never, let an employee or any establishment, or any man for that matter, get the upper hand (my mum told me that). As I stepped off the bus, just before it pulled away, the conductor shouted out, 'Go back home,' sticking his two fingers in the air. I held my nose in the air and with a straight back tried to stroll calmly down the road as though I hadn't heard him. I wasn't going to lower myself by following his example. Some adults.

As soon as I opened the front door I could sense the difference in the air. In the passageway, before I even reached the dining-room door, I knew that Mama Tiny had come.

'Well, Pastor Brown did gree bout it, an well, yu know wid one ting an anudda we is fambily,' said Mama Tiny.

'Hi, Mama Tiny,' I said, throwing my arms around her neck. She kissed my cheek and hugged me to her.

'Hi, Mum,' I walked over and planted a kiss on her cheek.

'Hello, darling. How was school?'

'Not too bad, I'm just finding it really boring. I can't wait for the term to finish.'

Mum was washing the rice in the sink with her back to me and I could tell from the way her shoulders were hunched that she had something to tell me, but didn't want to say it in front of Mama Tiny. Mama Tiny said it for her.

'Kiesha, remember de time we did talk bout mi coming to live wid yu all? Well, mi decide fi come,' she gushed out.

'Arrrghh, that's really great.' I screamed out. 'When?' I looked at Mum and I knew, then, that that was what she had wanted to tell me, because her shoulders had relaxed and she turned around.

'Next week,' she smiled.

I smiled too. But inside me something was happening. I started to think about my room and I had really to force the thought out of my mind for the moment.

'Oh, Mama Tiny, I'm so glad you're coming. I'll help you to move all your things and I'll help you to move into my room, I mean your room. It's gonna be really great

46

having you with us.' I beamed. I really meant it, but it was a bit hard to put into words. It was like I wanted it to happen and then again I didn't. Like going away on holiday: you can't wait to get there, and when you finally do, you feel homesick and uncomfortable but, give it a few days, you get so into things that you don't want to come home! Life is really funny. (Not funny ha, ha, but funny peculiar.)

Mama Tiny looked as though she was going to cry. She did.

'I'll be leavin Hosea behind,' she whispered. She held her face in her hands.

'Oh, Mama Tiny, don't cry,' said Mum quickly, drying her wet hands on the tea towel. Then, as she walked towards Mama Tiny with outstretched arms, she too began to cry. Oh well, I thought, I might as well join in, but then I couldn't help myself.

Then Mama Tiny said, 'Yu will never see yur fadda and yur grandfadda again,' looking from Mum to me. All three of us stood, stooped or sat in the kitchen, bawling our eyes out.

People (namely adults) say that after a time the pain goes away – when you miss someone you love. Well, it's been a year and it could have been yesterday as far as I'm concerned, I still miss Grandfather.

After supper Mum took Mama Tiny home with promises of help in sorting out all the things that she wanted to bring with her and the things that were going to be stored in Uncle Tim's and Uncle Stanley's houses. Mama Tiny said that she didn't want anything of hers going to Aunt Audrey's house. She didn't come out and say why but we all knew. Aunt Audrey was so into image and she'd imagine that just the sight of all that old furniture and bits and pieces being carted into her house would send the price of the house down!

I lay on my bed looking up at the ceiling. Goodbye ceiling. I looked over at the walls. Goodbye walls. The tree outside my window, which was really only the branches hanging over from next-door's tree, was a stop-over for so many birds; I would miss their company. I felt tearful. I felt like a baby. I took a deep breath. 'I'm only going next door,' I said to two pigeons pecking at each other, 'I'm not off to Timbuktoo, you know.' I was angry with myself for being so stupid about leaving my room. Then I felt guilty for not seeing it from Mama Tiny's point of view. She was leaving so many years of her life in that house, where my mum and my aunts and uncles grew up (well, for part of their lives, some of them spent the earlier part in Jamaica). The memories of Grandfather were on every strip of wallpaper, every stroke of paint (he did all the decorating himself). It must be heartbreaking for Mama Tiny to have to leave all that behind to live in one room (even though it was a reasonable size) and to have the rest of her belongings scattered in different houses. Now that made me sit up. I was only moving along the passage, with *all* my bits and pieces, and MJ was coming too. I supose I should count myself lucky and the bonus was that Mama Tiny was coming to live with us.

That'll be one over Renita and Patrice! Imagine if Mama Tiny was going to live at their house, I wouldn't be able to see her often at all, because I don't really like going over there. Renita (who is going to be just like her mother) would be calling her Grandmother, or Nanny, when she felt like being treated like a spoilt baby (which she is as far as I'm concerned). Patrice is okay, but if she has a 'funny turn' you just can't communicate with her. Then there's Aunt Audrey and, to tell you the truth, she's the main reason why we hardly visit the house. She's an awful woman, to put it mildly. I wondered if she really liked herself. I don't know that she does, otherwise why does she try to talk all posh and walk around her house as

48

though she's on the *Dallas* set, draped in silks and wearing high-heeled shoes? She is one hundred per cent PVC. I think she also has a touch of anorexia. She's constantly on a diet and when she is the rest of the family are too, and I think that's the reason Patrice sometimes gets all spotty. When she can only get celery or lettuce to eat at home she goes out and has chips or pie and mash or crisps to fill up on. My mum says that it's wicked to impose your ideas and your lifestyle on your children. I didn't say much to that as I wanted to remind her that when she was inclined to, she did the same to me. But that brings me to another annoying thing about adults: it's so easy for them to point out the mistakes that other people make, but if *you* tell them about a mistake that *they've* made, well, they want to kill you for it. It's really peculiar!

Oh well, I suppose I had better start sorting through my things. I had thought lately about clearing out some of my junk – well, now I had a reason for doing it.

Six

'Oh Kiesha, please say you can come,' begged Janeese, hanging on to my arm.

'I don't know what my mum will say. I can't just say yes, I'll have to ask her.'

I hoped that Mum would say yes. It isn't often that I am invited to a party, so I couldn't see any reason for her to say no, but with my mum it all depends on how I have been, if I have done my homework, or any housework she has given me, how she's feeling (you know, *that* time of the month) and anything else she can find to use as a reason for stopping me doing something or going somewhere. Well, that's not strictly true, but it does seem as if whenever I want to do something important like go to the school club she says I have to come home and do my homework – boring.

I really wanted to go to the party. Janeese had shown me a picture of her brother, who was seventeen, just. I had to say (and I'm a good judge of boys) he was really, really good-looking. But the unbelievable and incredible thing was that he and my Jamal were friends! Isn't that amazing? It seems that even though Janeese's family had lived on the other side of London and only recently moved over here, her brother already knew a lot of the boys (and girls, apparently) that went to my school. So, there were going to be lots of people from my school going and I definitely wanted to make sure that I was there too.

I had invited Janeese home after school one evening for supper. I really wanted Mum to meet her and give her approval to my choice of friends. She would no doubt give her the third degree, to see what kind of home she came from and whether she was the right sort of person for me to be mixing with. You would have thought I was bringing home a boyfriend the way Mum carried on. I knew Mama Tiny would like her. She had moved in a couple of days before and I had been telling her all about Janeese, you know, that I was sure she was underfed she was so skinny! I told her how Janeese sometimes came to school with a tear-stained face, because her parents had spent half the night fighting, which usually upset the whole household, and that from what I could gather and the way Janeese was behaving, she was on the way to becoming a nervous wreck.

'What a poor chile ee,' sighed Mama Tiny, after I had told her the latest concerning Janeese and her family. 'Yu must be kind to de poor ting, and treat her good, Kiesha, yu hear?' pointing her finger.

50

'Of course I'm nice to her. She's really lucky to have found such a sympathetic and generous friend as *me*' I pointed to myself to emphasise my answer. I don't know why I never went into any great detail when I told Mum anything about Janeese, perhaps it was because I didn't want Mum to think that I was fretting about her and Dad. Funny that, one minute I'm thinking whether or not they care about me and then the next thing is I don't want to cause them unnecessary worry.

As Janeese and I walked in the front door after school, we could smell the carrot cake that Mama Tiny, no doubt, had been baking. Mama Tiny, Janeese and I sat around the dining-room table sipping steaming hot Milo and eating carrot cake that had just been taken out of the oven. It was really cosy. When Janeese first met Mama Tiny she was all quiet but Mama Tiny soon got her to open up. Well, I never knew the girl could rabbit so much. She was like a symphony orchestra, gathering momentum for the great finale when the cymbals crash at the end. She told Mama Tiny (even though I was there I felt a bit left out, 'cos it seemed to me that if I wasn't it wouldn't have made much difference) all about her parents and how it seemed that they argued over stupid things that made no sense. Like the time her mum had taken some chicken from the freezer by mistake and cooked it for dinner and when her dad came home he really kicked up a stink because he said that they only had chicken on Sundays and today (that particular day was Tuesday) he wanted fish and he wasn't eating chicken so early in the week again. So Janeese's mum said, 'That's too bad, starve,' and dished it out for the children and herself. Janeese said that her dad was like someone who had got a sparkler shoved in his earhole (she could be quite funny when she wanted to – obviously she picked it up from me) and was ranting and raving about how inconsiderate her mum was, he had just come home from work and was tired and hungry while Janeese's mum

51

calmly carried on eating her dinner. Janeese said that she couldn't eat anything, she was a bit scared. Then her dad picked up the pot with the chicken in by the sides instead of the handle, it burned his fingers, he dropped it on his foot and the hot gravy went through his trousers, scalding his leg.

'Narena, Narena,' he shouted (that's Janeese's mum's name – unusual but nice), 'Narena, yu an yur mudda curse me, eh. Is yu do dis,' he wailed, leaping about like a frog. Janeese went on to say that her mum started to laugh, she threw back her head and tears were in her eyes because she was laughing so much. Janeese said that all through this she couldn't move, but when her mum started to laugh she could see the funny side of it and was dying to laugh, but if she had, her dad would have accused her later of taking her mum's side and he would've probably had a go at her.

That's another thing. Her dad always wanted her to take his side in any happenings between him and her mum. He didn't seem to mind what her brother did, but he wanted Janeese to take his side, always. When Janeese began to tell us about her dad, I felt sorry for her; if only her dad was like mine. I was trying to work out whether or not her dad liked her and whether she liked him. She spoke softly and hung her head as though she didn't want Mama Tiny to read her mind. Mind you, she soon cheered up when Mama Tiny offered her some more carrot cake, and it was such a large slice I couldn't believe it when she just took two bites and it disappeared down her throat. She's a regular little gannet. It's really funny you know. It seems as though you get a certain impression of someone when you only see them in a particular situation, but let that situation change and it's like you get a new person, you see things in them that they never revealed before. Whew! That Janeese with her pin legs and rake body was really a dark horse underneath that prim and proper, butter-wouldn't-melt-in-her-mouth disguise. She certainly had me fooled.

Mum came through the door with two full shopping bags from Sainsbury's. My dad used to say that Mum lived in that shop and must've had shares in it the way she bought their goods. In her hand she had a Pineapple and Mandarin Pavlova. Hmm, she was in a good mood.

'Hello everyone. Hello, you must be Janeese,' she smiled.

'Yes I am. Good evening, Mrs Ferell,' she said, standing up and holding out her hand for Mum to shake.

'Oh, oh good evening love.' Mum nearly dropped the pavlova in her haste to shake Janeese's hand. Well, I knew that that handshake clinched it right there and then. I would get an earful after Janeese had gone home about 'What a lovely polite girl she is' from Mum and Mama Tiny would probably say something like 'I coulda love de lickle chile like mi own', which would set off pangs of jealousy in me. I really felt like I was a spectator or someone watching TV, thinking I'm supposed to be in that situation, but it's like I've been forgotten. I felt sorry for myself.

'Kiesha, lay the table and then you can help me get the food ready,' Mum said.

'Yes, Mum,' I sighed. That's all I'm good for, work!

'What's wrong with you, young lady?'

'Nothing.'

'Well, stop showing off then and get a move on. Janeese will have to go home soon, we haven't got all night.'

It's at moments like these that I'm glad I'm an only child. The aggravation it must cause when there's more than one child, jostling to get their mum's attention – it must be more trouble than it's worth. I felt like Orphan Annie. I mean, I do feel sorry for her, her parents not getting on and all that, her brother not understanding her, her feelings of lonelinesss, but I felt like jumping up and saying, I feel just like that sometimes as well. I feel like pig-in-the-middle and Little Bo Peep, wandering around like a little boat lost at sea, but then I'll probably be told that my parents have already sorted out their differences and are now separated, and my dad comes round nearly every week to take me out and buys me presents – big deal!

Well, the only good thing that came out of Janeese's visit was that I could go to the party. Whoopee! I didn't have to grovel to Mum, she just said yes when Janeese asked her. Now that Mum had said I could go, I didn't feel too hard towards Janeese, as she had done her job of softening her up, but I don't think I will be too quick in the future to let her come round again!

There was one small drawback about going to Janeese's party (well, not hers, her brother's) which was that Patrice and Renita had to come too! I could've screamed. I didn't want them traipsing behind me, especially Renita, who thought that she was God's gift to boys and that once any boy had seen her, he was hooked for life (she was sick). There was one other matter that I didn't want exposed – I had told them that Jamal Hinds was my boyfriend. Well, he nearly is, I mean, the way he looked at me and smiled and once, when I was looking out of the chip-shop window during school lunchtime, he walked past and blew me a kiss. I nearly collapsed and had to hold on to the counter and I accidentally upset the wally bowl and all the vinegar spilt on me. I went back to school smelling all vinegary and Mum went crazy when I got home, but it was worth it!

I had heard a rumour which was so malicious it couldn't be true. The story was that my ex-friend Stacey was 'sort of' dating Jamal. I say that it's malicious as the person who told me was Beacon Wallis of all people and he is such a bare-faced liar. Like once I asked him the time (my mistake) and he told me it was half an hour later so I ran all the way to my lesson 'cos I thought I was late, and I could have taken my time. A right screwball! The other thing was that Stacey knew that I fancied him and that he was out of bounds for her, and I can remember how she said he was horrible and not her sort, he was *too* good-looking and, that being the case, he would have all the girls after him and she couldn't stand it. She said that he was far too old for me anyway, and why didn't I find someone who was more my age?

When I thought of all that she had said and now she fancied him herself, I could have screamed. How was I going to front it out with Patrice and Renita? I just didn't know. I wondered if I should ask Mama Tiny.

I had asked Mum if I could have this leather mini-skirt that I had seen in a shop in the high street to go with my leather jacket to wear to the party. She said that she'd have to see. Unfortunately her 'seeing' took so long, as it sometimes does, that the day of the party came and I still hadn't got my skirt. I was getting really desperate. I was seeing my dad that day, so I decided I'd have to work on him.

When he beeped on the horn as usual, I was out of the door like a flash and in his car – I didn't want to waste any time. As we were driving along I told my dad the latest about Janeese and her parents. He oohed and aahed and then I reminded him of her brother's party that evening and that Stacey, Patrice, Renita and Jamal were going.

'Who's Jamal?'

'I've told you millions of times, Dad, who Jamal is. He's a sixth former at my school and he likes me. He happens to be a friend of Janeese's brother and he's going to be at the party.' I smiled.

'What's a sixth former doing with a girl as young as you? I'll have to come and see your mother and ask her what she's doing sending you to school that has boys as old as men going there,' he shouted.

Now I knew I was treading dangerous waters. I

sometimes wish that when I have said something I shouldn't have, I could somehow erase those words. This was such a time. I didn't realise that Dad would see the situation in completely the wrong way and I didn't want him going and upsetting Mum, that would be terrible.

'Oh, Dad, it's nothing like what you think.'

'Well, young lady, what do I think?' he said gently.

I knew Dad was testing me so I thought I'd better think before I spoke.

'I, hmm, I think that you think I'm thinking that what you're thinking is not what I'm thinking and I . . .'

'That's enough hedging around the subject. I'll tell you what I'm thinking. I don't want my baby daughter having babies of her own.' He looked me square in the eye.

'Oh, Dad,' I wailed, 'how could you think of such a thing? I haven't even kissed him yet, he doesn't really know that I exist,' I pouted.

'Well, I'm glad to hear it. You can tell him from me, if he lays a hand on you, I'll come up to the school and kill him with my bare hands.'

Dad was fuming as he drove along the high street. I thought that he was going to knock down this old lady and her dog crossing the road. I didn't even feel safe with my seat belt on.

Anyway, he did calm down enough for me to persuade him to buy me the leather skirt. I didn't try it on in the shop as it was quite short and Dad would probably have had a fit and said I couldn't have it and I had tried it on six times before in the shop, so I knew what it looked like on. Mind you, Dad kept saying that there wasn't much leather in the skirt and was I sure that it would fit me!

Patrice and Renita came round as soon as I got in. You should have seen what Renita was wearing – she thought she looked like the girl Doris in *Five Star*, she should be so lucky. Patrice was wearing trousers as usual. I wanted to take my time getting ready, but with the two of them in my little bedroom it was impossible. Patrice kept going on about the length of my skirt so much that Mum was on the verge of telling me to take it off and find something else to wear. I was getting angry. In the car Mum gave us instructions about not drinking alcohol or smoking and went on about how terrible it all was, and that we must be good and stick together. I was thinking that as soon as I got inside I was splitting up from those two.

Mum pulled up outside Janeese's house and as we got out of the car we could feel the beat of the music on the pavement, it was so heavy. I could see that Mum was in two minds whether or not to come in with us.

'You'll be all right now, girls?'

'Yes, we will,' we said.

'Phone me if you want to come home before I come and get you at 1.30.'

'Okay Mum, we will,' I said over my shoulder as my legs took me in the direction of the music. I could hardly wait to get inside.

We walked into the passage and the music, the heat, the bodies pressed together, all hot and sticky, were a bit overwhelming at first. I found it difficult to catch my breath and what with the excitement of the whole evening in front of me it was too much. I felt like passing out.

'Hey fly girl' bellowed this voice from somewhere in the room with the music, where it was so dark I couldn't see. I didn't think it was for me or Patrice and especially not Renita, so I didn't take any notice.

> Hey sugar sweet
> You look good enough to eat

said the voice again. By now Patrice, Renita and I, and the girls around us, had started to giggle. Well, it was funny – who could be saying such nice things to us or at least to one of us? The music stopped and then the microphoned voice said:

> Baby, baby you're my fly girl
> Shake your tail, c'mon give me a whirl
> You're so sweet and you're my toy
> Baby Babe, I'm gonna be your house boy.
> Boom boom ba ca ba ca ba ca boom
> Do do do da, do do HEY
> Boom boom ba ca ba ca ba ca boom
> Do do do da, do do HEY.

Someone turned the music on again and the bass gave out some heaviness that ate right into your body. It must have affected everyone, because arms flew into the air, knees were bent down to the floor, heads were flung back and whistles were being blown, it was wild. Then the voice again:

> Hey fly girl in the leather suit
> You look sweet and ripe like cherry juice
> You can be my girlfriend, you surely can
> Because I'm gonna be your lover man
> HIT ME . . .

I was busy getting on down, shaking my body, throwing my arms and legs all over the place, just really getting on *down*. I felt that my blood was going to burst through my skin. I didn't cotton on that the boy on the microphone meant *me*. Patrice tapped me on the shoulder.

'Hey Kiesha, I think that boy means you.'

'What's the matter?' I said breathlessly.

'You, the boy's talking about you.' She pointed into the dark room. All I could see was bodies slithering about.

'I don't understand what you mean.' I carried on dancing.

'Kiesha,' Patrice held my arm. 'The boy who's talking on the microphone about his fly girl is talking about *you*,' she shouted above the music. I felt embarrassed, because people started to look at me.

'Come on, let's find out who this mystery boy is,' said Patrice, pulling my arm. I sort of hung back, everything was moving too fast for me. I wasn't really prepared to meet this boy. Who could he be? That reminded me I must find out where Jamal was.

'I don't particularly want to see who this "mystery" boy is, especially as, if he's talking about Kiesha, he obviously has something wrong with him,' said Renita. She's such a replica of her mother, she really makes me heave.

'Well, I think it would be nice to find out who he is,' I said over my shoulder as I followed Patrice.

My little fly girl has flown home to me
I'm gonna be your king, you're gonna be my queen.

As Patrice and I pushed through the crowd with Renita following reluctantly, my heart started to beat quickly. All of a sudden I felt weak at the knees. I pulled Patrice's arm, 'I don't think I can go through with this. What if he's talking about someone else who happens to have on a leather suit?'

Step right up, bo bo ba do
C'mon my little queen,
Hey let her through.

Patrice looked round to me: 'See, it is you.'

I felt sick, who could this person be? He sounded as though he had an American accent, but then I knew that whenever the boys were rappin, they all seemed to speak as though they came from New York, so that was no help. My mind was churning over wondering who it could be, when I thought of Jamal. The more we pushed through, the more I thought, yeah, that's who it is, it's Jamal. I couldn't think of anyone else who fancied me, especially talking like that about me. My heart shot right up inside my head, and I thought my head was going to pop off. I pulled Patrice's arm. 'Patrice, Patrice, I think it's Jamal.'

'Oh, wow, really? I can't wait to meet this boy who fancies you. He must need his head seeing to, especially if he's good-looking.' She was like a battering ram, elbowing her way through sweating bodies, following the little stream of light that the boys playing the music use to read the labels on the records. We stumbled into a pile of records that were on the floor by the turntable. When we'd recovered from that, I searched the faces eagerly for Jamal. Then I saw the microphone lead and slowly, with a big smile, I lifted my head to look fully into *his* face!

'Hey sugar sweet,' he oozed. Those teeth, those eyes, that grin, that idiotic grin did not belong to Jamal. I felt my heart, which a moment ago was popping out of my head, sink rapidly back down to my toes. I felt like running away. That ugly face belonged to none other than Beacon Wallis. He grinned. I felt sick.

Patrice said to him, 'Hi, Jamal, pleased to meet you. I'm Kiesha's cousin, Patrice, and that girl behind Kiesha is Renita, my sister. Hmmm, you're as handsome as she said. What's a good-looking boy doing with a girl like my cousin? You obviously have low standards.'

Then Renita leapt over my shoulder, just like the cow who jumped over the moon, and thrust out her hand to him. 'Please to meet you,' she said in her Aunt Audrey with a touch of Lady Di voice. 'So-o, you're the handsome beau in Kiesha's life, do you suffer from poor eyesight?' she beamed, showing all her gums. It's funny how in times of emergency your mouth loses its power, but another part of your body, say your hand, comes to your defence. In this case it was my foot. It just shot out into the

60

back of Renita's calf muscle of its own accord!

'Ouch, Kiesha, you've just kicked me,' she wailed.

I could sense that my hand wanted to follow suit, but I had to control it or who knows what could happen?

'Really,' I said sarcastically.

Beacon Wallis blew me a kiss. 'Thought it was Jamal Hinds, did you? I thought you fancied him, now I know for certain, ha, ha,' he laughed. I poked my tongue out at him. It was a good thing for him that I wasn't closer, otherwise he would have got my uncontrollable hand across his lips!

What an anticlimax. I tried to turn round so that I didn't have to face Beacon Wallis or my cousins, but there was no escape.

'Well, aren't you going to dance with him or give him a kiss or something?' said Renita.

I looked her right in the eye and felt like doing the 'something' to her but I inhaled deeply instead.

'Why don't *you* kiss him?' I hissed.

'It's not me that he fancies. Mind you, I'm sure if he got to know me he would forget all about you,' she cooed, looking at Beacon with funny eyes.

'Er, ladies, would you like some refreshments?' he grinned.

Now, I have never trusted Beacon and I knew that I never would.

'No thanks, we can get our own refreshments without your help.' I began to push through the crowd, trying to get out of the door. I didn't care whether Patrice or Renita were behind me; in fact, I hoped they weren't.

'Kiesha, you're here,' shouted Janeese from up the stairs.

I looked up and I couldn't believe my eyes. Janeese had her hair out loose, with the front caught up in a pony-tail and pulled over to the side of her head. She had on a black puff-ball skirt with a tight-fitting gold strapless top and a heavy gold-coloured necklace, and I had to look twice, because she had make-up on. I had to admit, though, she looked almost as good as me!

'Janeese, you look lovely. If you hadn't called out my name I wouldn't've known it was you.'

I could see she was pleased with what I had said.

'You look nice too.'

'Come here.' I beckoned to her.

She came down and we went to the kitchen. I guessed the two grown-ups we found there were Janeese's parents.

'Mum, Dad, this is my good friend Kiesha from school.' She held my arm.

'Hello,' nodded her dad to me.

'What a pretty girl,' said her mum, giving me a hug. 'Janeese has told me all about you, how she met your grandmother and your mother and how nice they were to her.' She kissed me on the cheek.

I felt close to her mum at once. She gave you the feeling that being close to her meant that no harm could come to you, as she would block its path. She reminded me a bit of Mama Tiny, but not quite, as I know that Mama Tiny is in a class of her own.

'Would you like something to eat?' she asked.

'Hmm, no thank you,' I smiled back.

'Would you like something to drink, then?'

'Yes please,' I said in my most polite speaking-to-grown-ups voice.

'I can see you have nice manners,' she beamed at me.

Janeese and I were standing sipping our drinks in the other room, as it was a little quieter than the room with the music. I told her all about what had happened, from Beacon Wallis calling me his 'fly girl' and 'ripe as cherry juice' and my thinking that it was Jamal, down to my kicking Renita in the leg. She said that she had heard all about it but she didn't realise it was me, because she didn't know that I had arrived.

I looked up, just as this really good-looking, unbeliev-
ably tasty (like the whole of the Jackson family – barring
MJ of course – rolled into one) boy (nearly man from
where I was standing) came into the room.

'Janeese,' he said.

I nearly collapsed. Who was this? Could it be Janeese's
boyfriend? But she'd never told me that she had one. I
could see why she hadn't, because from the way he was
looking at me, I could tell that he liked what he saw. What
a sneaking, selfish . . .

'Yes Neal,' she said.

'Mum said where have you put the other paper cups?'

'I put them in the cupboard under the sink.'

I was flabbergasted. I couldn't believe my eyes. He
turned and walked out of the door before I had chance to
say a word.

'Ja-Ja-Janeese,' I stammered. 'Who was that?' I pointed
as his back disappeared down the passage.

'Oh, him, that's Neal, my brother. I should've introduced you both.'

'Well, it's not too late now, is it?' I marched out of the
kitchen and made my way to the room that I had seen Neal
go into, with Janeese behind me. I pushed her forward.
'Go on,' I whispered. I felt a bit shy all of a sudden,
especially under the glare of the 100-watt light bulb.

'Neal,' Janeese called.

He turned around. 'Yeah, what?'

'This is my friend, Kiesha.'

'Oh right, nice to meet you, about time too. Janeese
keeps going on about her friend Kiesha, but we have never
had the chance to meet.' He held out his hand.

'Me too,' was all I could say. I shook his hand.

'You'll have to come round here more often, so that we
can get to chat, okay?' he smiled.

I nearly fainted. 'Yeah, sure.'

I felt as though I was being overtaken by that very strong force called LOVE. I could just about control myself. All this excitement in one night was too much even for a young girl like me.

I pulled Janeese's arm. 'Why didn't you tell me that your brother was so delicious.'

'Is he?'

'"Is he?" she says. He's dynamite. Look, has he got a girlfriend?' I asked.

'Well, no, not really, he has girls who are friends, but not anyone special.'

'Oh, Janeese,' I hugged her. 'This is the moment I've been waiting for. Right, this is what I want you to do for me.' I explained to her that she had to wangle it so that her brother and I got together again.

'Oh Kiesha, what about Jamal?'

'Who?'

No sooner was the word out of my mouth when who should put his head into the room but Jamal Hinds. He had on a leather suit, and the trousers were really tight, just how Prince wears them. Wow! I leaned against the wall. My mind was buzzing. All these boys and I had to choose!

'Hello, Kiesha Ferell. Fancy seeing you here.'

I focused my eyes on the face whose mouth had just spoken.

'You look as though you've just seen a ghost, he he.'

'Oh, it's you, Stacey Bailey, and I see you've got Gail in tow as usual. What are you doing here?'

She grinned (just like the cat that she is). 'More's the question, what are you doing here?'

I lifted my head in the air as though talking to her was a waste of time. 'Well, hmm, I was invited by the host, we're really good friends.'

'Really. Jamal brought me.' She held his arm.

My face turned to stone, so that she couldn't see that what she had said was like a knife in my heart. Oh Jamal, I thought, how could you do this to me? I had to put up a brave front.

'Really? If he brought you, he must feel sorry for stray cats,' I said, then turned to talk to Janeese in order to restrain myself – I felt like hitting her.

'Jamal, do you want a drink?' purred Stacey.

'It's all right, I'll get them. The usual, girls?'

They both nodded.

He was walking towards the door when suddenly he stopped and turned to Janeese and me. 'Do you want a drink, Janeese, Kiesha?'

'Oh, yes please,' I said, before Janeese could answer.

My hero, he has just rescued me.

I stood looking at the pair of them. Huh, look at them, I thought, wolves in sheep's clothing. Well, I've got Janeese now, so you're both welcome to each other. With the reputation that Streaky Bacon has, Stacey must be just as bad by now. Good, they deserved each other. Jamal brought our drinks back and said he wanted to stand near the sound system, so he went to the other room.

It was after one in the morning. I could see Stacey and Streaky looking cheesed off, probably wondering where Jamal was. I wanted to laugh, serves them right, how could those horrible girls ever think that someone as good-looking as Jamal would be interested in them?

'Kiesha, your mum's at the door,' Patrice shouted into the room.

'Who has to run home to mummy, then?' laughed Stacey.

Big mouth Patrice, why couldn't she just come up and whisper it to me instead of bellowing it out like a town crier!

'Tell her I'm coming.' I turned to Stacey. 'It just so happens that my mum loves me.' I turned back to Janeese. 'See you later, and thanks.' Then I whispered to her:

65

'When shall I come over and see your brother?'

She looked thoughtful for a moment. 'How about next Saturday?'

'I can't, I go with my dad then. Look, phone me tomorrow, okay?' I looked at her.

'All right.' She nodded her head. 'I'm glad we're friends.' She squeezed my hand.

'Yeah, so am I.' I grinned at her.

As I walked towards the car I felt good inside that I would be able to have the first offer of Neal for a boyfriend because of Janeese being my friend.

Patrice and Renita were already in the car.

'What took you so long Kiesha?' asked Mum.

'Oh, I was saying bye to Janeese's parents.'

'Did you have a nice time girls?'

'Marvellous,' I said.

'Interesting,' replied Patrice.

'Boring,' yawned Renita.

Seven

'At last mi find one lickle church, mi know seh di Lawd want mi fi go an praise im dere,' smiled Mama Tiny, sitting down at the table. She kicked off her shoes and took off her hat and rested it on the table.

'Mama Tiny, you going to start this Sunday?' asked Mum.

'But of course, yu never tink seh mi walk all bout fi look a church an mi nar gwine go?'

Mum filled the kettle up. 'I know that you're going to go but I thought you might want to rest until next week.'

66

Mama Tiny blew her nose and began to look through her bag. 'Mi dear. Even though mi old yu tink seh mi is feeble.' She kissed her teeth. 'Yu see mi,' she pointed to herself, 'mi lickle but mi tallawah. Mi even tink seh mi ave more strengt den yu,' she pointed at Mum, who smiled. She knew it was no use arguing with Mama Tiny; when her mind was made up that was that and only a fool continued to argue with her.

'Kiesha,' said Mama Tiny putting on her glasses and then looking at me over the rim. 'I ave someting fi yu.' I couldn't tell from her tone of voice what she was up to. I had come to learn that when Mama Tiny thought something was good for you, you might not agree with her and what was worse, you couldn't tell her so.

'Yes, Mama Tiny?' I looked up from the book I was reading at the table. Mama Tiny held out a package for me.

'Come an see what yur grandmudda bring fi her lickle grandpicknee.' She smiled and her top dentures almost, but not quite, fell down.

With mixed feelings, I took the package. It was a book. Great! I loved to read and Mama Tiny had bought me two books already. One was *The History of Jamaica* – really boring stuff, but it looked impressive on the bookshelf – and the other was *The Color Purple*, which was a bit difficult to understand, but I really enjoyed it until she asked me what it was about and I couldn't really put it into words, so I told her I would have to read it again. I was trying to persuade Mum to let me go to the pictures to see it, so that I might understand it a bit better.

I untied the package. It was the Bible. Oh boy, I wonder why she's bought me this. 'Oh, thank you, Mama Tiny, but I've already got one.'

'What yu mean, you nar want dis one den?' she enquired.

'Oh yes, I do, I was only saying,' I said quickly.

She smiled at me. 'I'm glad,' she said.

My face fell. Oh, no. I know she's up to something, I just know that there is more to come. It came all right.

'I ave noticed dat on Sunday, which as yu know is de Lawd's day, yu nar seem fi do anyting, except plabba plabba pon de telephone, and lydung bout de place like yus big ooman, moresomever, yuself an yur mudda nar respect de Lawd's day. Well, yur mudda big fi know her own mine, an anyway she did raise up wid mi auntie in countree, so mi understan, but yu chile' – she looked at me from my head to my toes – 'need some edication bout de Lawd an im ways.' She must've seen my expression: 'Me know seh yu nar gwaan tank me now, but when yu turn big smaddy, yu will be sooo happy dat me tek yu inna hand, an guide yu. So on Sunday yu will come a church wid mi, all right darlin?' She smiled sweetly at me, bent over and picked up her bag and went trotting up the stairs.

'Mum,' I exploded, 'I don't want to go to church. Tell Mama Tiny that I don't want to go.'

'Oh, Kiesha, it's not that bad. I used to go with Stanley and Audrey and Tim. We were all right, we used to have a great time, I was even in the choir. Anyway, sometimes as you get older the time spent in Sunday School comes in useful. I know that at times the only person you can turn to is Jesus, because at the time perhaps friends can't help you, your family don't understand and Jesus just seems to come to the rescue. Actually, I've been meaning to take you from ever since you were small, but in a way I'm glad Mama Tiny's taking you.' She smiled down at me, holding out her arms. I got up from the table and walked over to her. She put her arms around me and I slipped my arms around her waist. It was nice standing in the kitchen like this. I realised that it was ages since Mum and I had been this close. We always seem to be arguing with each other. It made me think that when you live with someone, even though you love them, you must end up arguing about something or other.

'Mum, do you still love Dad?' I could've bitten my tongue, how could I let something so dangerous out? I held my breath.

Mum said nothing at first, then: 'Kiesha, what can I say? When you have lived with someone you love, that person becomes part of you. You join together to make a little one like you, you share together in good times and bad and then things just seem to get out of hand, neither of you can control the situation and you just grow apart. The thing is that all that went on before doesn't go away and all kinds of emotions that you weren't even aware of seem to manifest themselves, especially when you don't want them to, and you can't seem to control them and it just tears you apart.' She breathed deeply. I squeezed her tighter. I could feel drops of salt water against my cheeks: Mum was crying. I felt a hollowness inside, I wasn't sure how I should be feeling. I was just numb. 'Yes,' Mum whispered, 'I do love your dad, but we just can't seem to make it.'

'Mum, I love you,' tumbled out.

She hugged me tighter to her.

'You'll always be my baby and I love you, I more than love you, I love love *love* you,' Mum said.

I floated up the stairs and knocked on Mama Tiny's door.

'Yes,' she called.

I popped my head around the door. 'I'll be coming on Sunday, Mama Tiny.'

'Hmm,' she said, drawing herself up to lean against the bedhead, 'I know.' I looked surprised. 'How do you know? I've only just made my mind up.'

'I just finish pray fi ask de Lawd fi encourage yu fi come, an look how de Lawd annsa mi prayer. Close de door behind yu.' She slipped down under the covers.

I slowly closed the door and walked to my room,

thinking how my old room had changed since Mama Tiny had taken it over. Instead of MJ on the wall there were pictures of Grandfather and my other relatives. There were plastic flowers all over the place, the room looked like a miniature Kew Gardens! Every inch of room was filled with something; it looked claustrophobic to me, but Mama Tiny seemed happy in it.

Lying with my hands behind my head and my knees bent, I thought about the last few hours. I couldn't really remember but it seemed such a long time since Mum and I had last kissed and hugged and felt close to one another. It must've been after Mum and Dad separated, but before we moved into this house, I thought, racking my brains. What a long time. It seemed so funny, everything was working its own way out. It was only a few days before that I had been thinking that Mum and I were far apart, she didn't seem to understand me at all, or she didn't want to understand. I mean, I had lost out not having my father near me. She had appeared concerned only about her own feelings, mine didn't seem to count.

I had discussed this very thing with Janeese, you know, the fact that whatever parents go through in their lives, they don't seem to be too bothered about how or what their children feel. Now, Janeese and I felt that that is really selfish. How can you be so insensitive to your children's feelings? I mean, they (parents) brought us into the world, we never asked to be, and sometimes the way they go on about it you would think that they have done us a favour! They think nothing of fighting and arguing in front of us and blatantly asking us to choose sides. Janeese said that only the other day her father (but then men and boys are a little creepy like that) was trying to bribe her with a pair of new shoes if she agreed that her mum was being unreasonable to him! Well, I ask you. You know, I felt a real dislike for him. My dad had never done anything like that. But then, wait a minute, I just remembered that

70

for a while, whenever he and Mum fell out, he would sneak up to my room and ask me, 'How was your day boolooloops?' (By the way, in case you were wondering, that means darling or sweetheart – and he called me or Mum this when he was: (1) grovelling, (2) seeking our attention, (3) up to no good, or (4) in a good mood. You then had to weigh up the situation and apply the number accordingly.) I had never thought about it in that way, but yes, my dad had been playing on my feelings. But I didn't fall for it, even though I didn't realise that it was happening at the time.

I wrapped my arms around my back. I love you, Mum, I breathed out softly. I could still feel Mum's body against mine, soft and solid, warm and secure. Poor Mum. She's so attractive, she always dresses smartly, she could have her pick of any bloke, yet she still loves Dad, I knew that now, and I was sure she had meant all she had said. How can you stop loving someone whom you have shared a large lump of your life with? Unless you have radical open-heart surgery, it's near impossible. I felt good inside.

Now, the next thing to find out was did Dad still love Mum? I hoped so, because then I could act as the mediator. I would have to talk to Mama Tiny about this. I knew that deep down she still had a soft spot for my dad. 'Lyndon, im is like a son an to tell de trute, im ave more sense dan Audrey osband, an mi like im de best.' I felt good when she said that. You can't blame her – most people feel the same about my dad.

I knew that Mama Tiny liked Uncle Robin but, as Mum put it, Aunt Audrey has castrated him! I had to look that up in a dictionary and the next time I saw him I kept looking, but you can't really tell, and I wanted to ask him, but I would have been embarrassed. Anyway, even if she did, they have got three children and that's enough. I think they should have stopped at Mervyn and not carried on to have Patrice and Renita. On the other hand, Mervyn is a bit funny, not funny hilarious, but funny strange. Whenever he's at home, he spends most of his time in his room (mind you, if I was in that family so would I) and when he isn't at home, he's away at college. Aunt Audrey is forever boasting about how intelligent 'her Mervyn' is and how he takes after her. I don't think so. Sometimes when Aunt Audrey is giving one of her 'speeches', if Mervyn's present he sits with his head down, shuffling his feet. I know he feels embarrassed about his mother. She's so thick-skinned. She's always spouting about what she thinks and what she's done, and people can be as sarcastic as they like, but it never seems to sink in!

Anyway, back to my dad. How could I get him into a frame of mind where I could ask him if he still loved Mum? Hmm, I'll have to try out this prayer business, to see if it works.

'Mum, I don't want to wear that hat,' I wailed. It was awful. It looked like a pink flower pot with a bit of fishnet sprouting out of the middle and (I don't know who designed it, it must've been for a joke) it had a bunch of pink and white cotton flowers on a stem with leaves! Mum seemed not to have heard me, as she went on fiddling with the hat on my head.

I looked up into her face, trying to get her attention, 'Mum, I don't need this hat, it looks silly.'

'No, it doesn't, I think you look quite sweet in it.' She stood back to get a good look at me. 'There,' she patted my cheek, 'you look gorgeous.'

'Well, I certainly don't feel it. I feel awkward, out of place.' My hands were itching to drag the hat off my head. It had been Mama Tiny's idea to wear a hat. Apparently, all the women wore hats to church: it was supposed to be written in the Bible that women had to. When I asked if men had to wear hats, the answer was no. You know, increasingly, I'm finding out that this is a man's world. They can go off and have all the fun and we women (well, I'll be one soon) have to take all the rubbish, leftovers and hand-me-downs. I'm certainly not going to put up with that when I get older. I'm no second-class citizen. But I was still stuck with the hat.

'What a way Kiesha look stylish, ee?' breezed in Mama Tiny, swishing her coat-tails, which matched her dress and hat. 'Now I can boast seh how dis young ooman a mi grandpicknee,' she beamed over at me. I gave her a plastic grin in return.

'Good, I see seh yu ready, now come, let's tek breeze.' She marched out of the house, without even looking behind her to see if I was there – she knew I would be.

Mum pushed me gently, 'Go on, or you'll be late.'

When we got off the bus I could hear singing from the other side of the predestrian crossing. As we walked towards the church I read the big blue and white sign which stretched from one side of the church wall to the other: THE EVANGELICAL CHURCH OF THE APOSTLES OF CHRIST. If it weren't for the singing, which sounded as though the people who sang were happy, the name alone would've frightened me.

Mama Tiny had been full of joy on the bus, telling me how pleased she was at finding a church that was so similar to the one she had to leave when she came to live with us. She had been shopping in Ridley Road Market when she had met an old friend of hers, Matilda Cassandra Shuttlebottom, Miss Mattie to everyone. Mama Tiny said that they both nearly walked past one another, but it was as though 'Dem spirit de touch' and they both spun round at the same time:

'But nar Miss Mattie dis, ee?'

'Ar oh, Mama is really yu, but stop, mi did hear seh how yu gawn home fi good,' she said. They both started to laugh and hug each other.

'No Miss Mattie, it nar trute, mi gawn live wid mi daughter an her chile. If mi did gawn home, mi woulda write an tell yu!'

They were so glad to see one another that they chatted for ages about this and that, and all around them people were busy doing their shopping and going about their business. Miss Mattie asked Mama Tiny if she was going to church now that she had moved.

'Well, I been looking an I cyaan find a church dat is rightly moving in de Lawd's spirit in true.'

Miss Mattie had told her about this one. She said that Sister Lucinda, her friend, went to this church and sang its praises and how the people were the true soldiers of the Lord!

As we walked into the church, there were a few people milling about in the entrance, greeting one another, shaking hands, nodding heads. I held on to Mama Tiny's hand. The church was a bit overwhelming for me, the building was so deceptive. Outside it seemed average sized, but once you got inside it was enormous.

We walked in past the usher, who gave us a hymn book and pointed out two vacant seats at the back of the church. Mama Tiny smiled and thanked him and walked in the opposite direction. She marched right up the front as though she was a queen. I tagged along behind trying to disappear inside my jacket collar.

Just as I was getting comfortable in my seat at the front the choir struck up a song and the whole congregation stood up.

The choir sang: Jesus the Lamb of God.
The congregation sang: Praise His name!
The choir sang: Jesus for sinners slain.
The congregation sang: Praise His name!
Everyone sang: Hallelujah, Hallelujah, Hallelujah.
Praise His name!
Then I heard a trumpet blow out notes that made you

74

feel you were listening to a record, followed by drums, electric guitars and tambourines, and everyone started to sing. It was the same few words, but boy, it changed the song completely. I wanted to dance. As I looked around me I could see that people were dancing, not as though they were at a party, but then again not far from it. Even Mama Tiny was in full swing. She had her eyes closed and was moving in time with the beat, clapping her hands. In fact everyone was moving, it was great. This was the last place that I'd thought you could really have a good time. I started to clap my hands and move to the music. It was raw and wild.

It went on for some time and I was ready to freak out like I did at Janeese's brother's party, when a loud voice rang out: 'Chosen saints, we come before the Lord.'

Instantly the music stopped, the singing stopped and I didn't even realise, I had got so carried away. Mama Tiny dug me with her elbow. I stopped jigging about.

The pastor coughed: 'Let us bow our heads.'

He seemed to pray for hours. People said 'Amen' and 'Hallelujah' throughout and generally agreed with what he was saying. My feet were aching, I was tired – I had hardly slept the night before because I was worried about what the church would be like. Now I wanted to go home.

'The reading today,' bellowed the pastor, 'is taken from Matthew Chapter 25, reading from verse one alternatively.' I found it a bit difficult to keep up because the Bible that Mama Tiny had given me was written in thous and thines. It was like reading a foreign language.

After the reading we had to stand up and sing again (that's when I came alive, I could shake off the tiredness that was nearly overtaking me). Then the tithes and offerings were to be taken. I didn't like the sound of that and was growing a bit apprehensive. When I asked Mama Tiny what was happening, she said that it was collection time. Why couldn't he have said that instead? I was a little suspicious about the people around me: it was as though they were in a different world. It was hard to look around at the other people because no one else seemed to be doing it, but out of the corner of my eye I thought I recognised one of the guitar players, a young man (or was it a boy?) who looked familiar. I was screwing up my eyes to try and get a positive look, when the pastor began to speak:

'Brethren,' he boomed. 'Are you ready?'

'Yes sir, we ready.'

'I've bin purchased.'

'Jesus my Redeemer.'

'Hallelujah.'

'Are you one of the Wise Virgins or are you one of the Foolish Virgins?' he barked and pointed his finger.

I held my breath. His eyes seemed to be piercing mine. I was afraid he had the power to look right inside me, at my thoughts, he even knew what I was thinking now! I froze. I tried my hardest not to think, so that he wouldn't know my mind, but my mind has a will of its own. Thoughts of starting my periods flooded my mind, of kissing MJ's picture on the wall, of wanting Jamal to hug me and imagining that I was married to him and having his children. Could this man see all that? Well, he must be able to see into everybody, that was why he was asking who was a wise or foolish virgin. I thought of Mama Tiny, I mean, look at all the children she had, why was this man being personal? I felt like saying something to him, I was surprised Mama Tiny hadn't.

'Have you enough oil in your lamp to keep it burning?' he shouted.

What was this man talking about – virgins, lamps and oil? Then it dawned on me: the passage of scripture. I felt my whole body relax. What a fright. I thought this man could read everyone's mind, mine in particular!

My feet were getting all pins and needle-ish. I had been sitting for too long. I looked at my watch – three hours

76

gone by, I must've fallen asleep.

'Evening service begins promptly at 6.30,' said the pastor.

Everyone began to get up and walk towards the door. What a relief. I couldn't see myself coming again. I did enjoy the music, but everything else was just too much. Mama Tiny got talking to a woman who had been sitting behind us.

'Dat man know how fi preach, ee?' said the woman.

'Yes, im speak de Lawd's word in trute. Im nar turn to de left or de right, but traight up de narrow path,' preached Mama Tiny, demonstrating with her arms.

We finally got to the door, after Mama Tiny had stopped to talk to everyone. I saw our bus go past. What a drag, my new shoes were really pinching my toes and I was hungry. Never again.

I went outside while Mama Tiny was talking and leant against the church wall. It was a warm day and the gentle heat of the sun touched my face. I closed my eyes and waited for Mama Tiny. It felt good to be out in the fresh air. A feeling of goodness began to well up inside me and I was glad to be alive.

A shadow fell across my face. Now I'm not at all superstitious, but I had a feeling that it wasn't a good sign. When I opened my eyes I found I was right. Beacon Wallis stood in front of me, flashing his teeth like his namesake at a zebra crossing. He was all dressed up in a two-piece suit. I must admit he did look smart, but there was no way I was going to tell him, especially after he had embarrassed me at Janeese's brother's party, showing me up in front of Patrice and Renita and everyone else for that matter. I really didn't want to talk to him. Then it occurred to me: what was a vile and wicked person like Beacon Wallis doing in church? I mean, I know that it's a good place for wicked people to come to get themselves sorted out, but I think he was past sorting!

'Oi, what you doing here, Ferell?' he grinned.

'None of your business. More to the point, what are you doing here?'

'I asked you first.' He leaned against the wall.

'What are you standing next to me for?' I moved along the wall to get away from him. 'Anyway, it's none of your business why I'm here.'

'I play in the band,' he said.

My mouth dropped open. I'd thought I recognised the face but I couldn't believe it was Beacon playing the guitar so well.

'I didn't notice you.'

'Too bad. Anyway, I knew you fancied Jamal Hinds. Well, I can tell you for nothing, he don't fancy you,' he laughed wickedly.

That was all I needed right now. Him digging the knife in. I knew that Jamal liked me just from the way he looked at me, I can tell these things, every woman can. Anyway, I liked Janeese's brother, Neal, so Jamal had missed his chance, but I wasn't going to tell Belisha Beacon that. Hmm, that was a good name for him, Belisha Beacon. I must tell Janeese.

'I liked your leather suit,' he smiled at me.

Words failed me. He was made of stone. After he had shown me up something rotten, he now had the gall to say that he liked my outfit. I straightened my back and looked him in the eye. 'Beacon Wallis, I find your manner somewhat insuffereable.' I had heard a woman on TV say that to some man who fancied her but she didn't fancy him. 'Furthermore, please do not make any reference to my appearance, because coming from your mouth it sounds horrible!'

He laughed. 'Pull the other one, Ferell. You're nothing but a jumped-up squirt.'

I turned my back on him. He tapped me on the shoulder.

'Are you a wise or foolish virgin?' He roared with laughter. 'I don't think you're anything, you're not even human.' He held his stomach and screamed with laughter at his own pathetic joke. I felt like kicking him, but it wouldn't have looked right in the church yard.

'Kiesha,' Mama Tiny called. 'Seh bye to yur young frien, yu can see im next week when yu come.'

I gave him a plastic grin, just for Mama Tiny's sake. If I didn't she would want to know why and get all involved.

I was standing at the bus stop wondering why Beacon Wallis, of all people, was in church, when a car with an oldish man and a boy in it pulled up. It was Beacon Wallis. It wasn't fair. I was going to have to learn the art of prayer, to get this parasite out of my hair. The old man leaned over and introduced himself as Mr Wallis, Beacon's grandfather, and asked us if we wanted a lift. Mama Tiny said yes. She told Brother Wallis all about herself, how she was a widow living with her daughter and that I was her granddaughter, and all the ins and outs of our family tree! Talk about this is your life, Eamonn Andrews couldn't have done a better job. I don't know why I was angry with Mama Tiny telling them everything, well, I do know. You see, Beacon Wallis is so spiteful, he would turn information from Mama Tiny around and throw it back in my face, especially if there were an audience, so that afterwards he could strut about like a prize peacock. Ugh! How I hated that boy. I had to find a way to get back at him.

They dropped us off right outside our house, and Mama Tiny asked them if they would like to come in for refreshments. I had to send up a prayer quickly.

'No thanks,' they said.

It was answered. I really would have to find out about this prayer situation.

They drove off with promises to pick us up whenever we wanted a lift. Thanks, but no thanks.

Eight

I hate cleaning my room. It is smaller than my other room and hasn't got built-in wardrobes, so I haven't got that much space. At least the window still overlooks the garden, but I miss the tree outside. Dad bought me one of those lampshades that you can pull up and down. Right snazzy! Well, I suppose I can't complain, I still have a bit of room between the window and my bed to dance! I don't know how I accumulate so much rubbish. I sorted through my drawers. 'Nothing but odd foot socks,' I said to myself. 'Where can the other foot to them be?' I hunted through the other drawers, finding just as much junk. I got so fed up that I just bundled everything back into the drawers and shut them tight. I hoped Mum wouldn't come checking in my drawers, she'd go mad when everything fell out.

I went over to the window taking Oliver, my teddy bear which I've had since I was three I reckon. He's so cuddly. He can keep secrets. He can't answer back, which I think is a bonus at times. He's a real gem.

We sat staring out of the window. Mum was out in the garden, pruning the flowers. She straightened up for a while, holding her back. 'I should really go down and help her, but I prefer to look out of the window and think,' I said to Oliver, who understood me completely.

Mum bent down again and began to dig. The sky didn't look too clear today, so much for summer. It's really strange, the weather. In fact it reminds me of people, just like the wind when it blows hot and cold. Some days you go out with just light clothing, summer tops and shorts, and after a while you have to run for shelter, because it's coming down in bucketfuls! As I said, just like people: you can be having a perfectly normal, reasonable conversation with someone and bang – they explode like a firecracker, for no reason. Very strange.

I thought about Jamal. Now, I know it seems like I'm jumping from one boy to another, but things aren't always what they seem. I do like Jamal. He's good-looking, nice personality (I know that as you get older, that counts more than looks), seems very generous, pleasant, but what is worrying me is the fact that he seems very friendly with Stacey Bailey and Streaky Bacon. But as far as I'm concerned, they're both creeps and if he is prepared to be friends with them, then out of all his good points I must've overlooked something. He must have something wrong with him to be friends with them. Then of course, he could just be feeling sorry for them and he lets them hang around him, hmm, you see, he is so sweet, that could be the explanation for it. But I don't know. It's not right. I mean, it doesn't seem a sensible thing to have something you don't like hanging round your neck! No, definitely not. I'll have to blow him out of my life. I mean to say, I don't want our marriage ending in divorce just because he feels sorry for undesirables and insists on having them around him. He might end up feeling *too* sorry for them! No, sorry, he'll have to go – but he's so good-looking. 'What do you think, Oliver? Blow him out?' (It's at times like these I wish Oliver could talk!)

Hmm, Neal, he really is the business. When I first saw him at the party, he nearly blew my socks off! He seems a bit quiet, but I personally find the quiet sort much more appealing. The only thing is, when I start going out with him, how is Jamal going to feel? I know he will feel really let down. This situation is like trying to get off a merry-go-round that won't stop! It's so hard being the centre of attention. I wonder how Madonna copes with it all. You know, jealousy is a terrible thing, it sometimes makes men do things they wouldn't normally do, like fight over a woman. Wouldn't that be terrible? What a mess.

I don't know where Mum gets all that energy from. The way she was mowing the lawn, it was like she was taking revenge on the grass. Up and down, up and down, moving like greased lightning. Hold on, she looks different. I screwed up my eyes to get a better look. I know what it is, she's lost weight, her jeans look a bit loose on her. But she hasn't been dieting, has she? What's going on? Oh well, she looks nice for it. I pressed my face against the window-pane and closed my eyes. I could almost feel the vibrating hum of the lawn mower. It was like when the dentist drills your teeth and the injection hasn't worked and you can feel the drill. It made my skin crawl.

I opened my eyes and there was Mama Tiny standing in the middle of the garden with her hands on her hips. Is she acting as a scarecrow or has she come to help Mum? She started to wave her arms about – wait a minute, that means trouble. Hold up, she and Mum are arguing, what's wrong? I couldn't make up my mind whether to sit up there and watch the fireworks or go downstairs and get a better view. But then, it depended on what they were arguing about. It could be me and then if I was downstairs I might cop the lot of their venom. But it could be something else.

'Oliver, what do you think I should do?' I asked the blank face of my teddy bear. Silence. 'Stupid (dumb) animal. I don't know why I put up with you, you're of no utter use to me.' I threw him across the bed. He just lay there like an over-stuffed toy!

I looked up at MJ, who just smiled. 'What do you

reckon Michael?' I knew the answer – he just carried on smiling, 'Yea, I'll go down and find out what's what.' I sighed as I made my way downstairs.

As I crept down the last few steps, I could just faintly hear their voices. I walked casually into the kitchen and made myself some orange squash, keeping my eyes fixed on Mama Tiny and Mum. I could hear them loud and clear, in fact I think the whole neighbourhood could.

'But yu is a married ooman, how can yu seh yu a galang wid man fi dinner, dat nar right. An what bout Kiesha, who will mind her when yu gawn, ee?' shouted Mama Tiny.

'Honestly, Mama Tiny,' said Mum, weeding a flowerbed, 'Kiesha is twelve years old, not two, she doesn't need looking after, she can look after herself. Besides, she can spend the night at Audrey's if you're unable to stay with her. Ian and I are only going out for a meal and Lyndon and I live separate lives, and Lyndon to my knowledge has not been living the life of a monk since we split up. Look at him, he has the cheek to drive up to my house with his concubine in the front seat, to pick up our daughter, without a care in the world! How come you don't comment on the way he's behaving?' She ripped out some flowers by mistake. 'Oh, look what I've done, and another thing,' she lowered her voice but I could still hear her, 'sometimes I think you would've preferred it if he was your son and I was your daughter-in-law the way you make me feel,' she hissed, and throwing down the shovel she stormed into the house.

I quickly tried to swallow the orange squash, to make it look as though I wasn't particularly interested in their quarrel, and at the same time smile at Mum rushing past me, but somehow or other the drink went down the wrong hole. I was seized with such a coughing fit I had to hang on to the edge of the sink, but I managed to call out to Mum, who turned around.

83

'Yes love,' she said.

'What's up, Mum?' I said, breathing unevenly.

'Oh, nothing for you to worry about. It's okay.' She tried to smile.

'How can things be okay, if you and Mama Tiny are rowing?'

She came over to me and cupped my chin in her hand. 'Take it from me, chicken. I've got everything under control,' she said, and walked out of the door.

I was still coughing my lungs up when Mama Tiny walked slowly into the kitchen. Her face seemed to have aged. She looked tired. She sat down at the table, put her head in her hands and sighed.

I went over to her and put my arms round her. 'What's up, Mama Tiny?'

'Nuttin wrong chile, just de usual pattern of life, wid its up an down.'

I pulled the chair nearer to her, so that we could be closer to each other. We sat in silence for a while. It seemed really quiet now that the lawn mower was off and Mama Tiny and Mum had stopped shouting at each other. Mama Tiny stirred in her chair. She turned to look at me. 'Kiesha,' she said, putting her hand under my chin, 'yur mudda is right. Yu are a big gal now, no point in hidin tings from yu. What we nar tell yu, some fas smaddy will.' She kissed me on the cheek.

I braced myself for whatever was coming. 'Chile, it's life, yu will soon be livin yur life, so jus put it down to experience, ee?'

She got up and put the kettle on. I wanted to say something, but I knew Mama Tiny's ways. When she has something to say, she toys around with it in her mind until she can put it delicately but straight to the point.

'Well, mi young granddaughter, yur madda ave one bwoyfriend, a tek her out dis comin Saturday, an if Ian,' she emphasised his name, 'is able fi get teatre seat, dem a

84

gu fi see one show or someting gu so. Hmm.'

'What? You're joking,' I shouted at Mama Tiny, making her jump. I felt ill. I mean, who does she think she is? Just like Dad – they are really alike, messing up all my plans, just when I was trying to work out a way to get her and Dad back together again. My face must've shown my feelings because Mama Tiny's turned to thunder.

'I tell yur madda its nar right what she a do, looking one man an yur fadda still alive. Yur grandfadda a turn inna im grave. Imagine, one a im picknee a sport a next man, no, it nar right,' she shouted.

Oh, Mum, I cried inside, why are you doing this? Tears started to roll down my cheeks, I felt so frustrated and hurt. I leaned on the table and buried my head in my hands. I felt Mama Tiny's strong bony arms encircle me.

'Hush now chile, so life gu. After all yur madda is a ooman, an she ave need of a man in her life.' She kissed the top of my head. I felt defeated, before I had even begun. Any reconciliation now seemed impossible. '. . . an den yur fadda ave one galfriend yur madda see im wid, im a come brazen up imself wid de gal, outside yur madda door. Nar wonder yur madda gwan do dis. Mi know seh dem both love one anudda, but dem both too high an mighty fi talk tings tru. Lawd, what a sinting a gwan inna mi fambily.' She kissed her teeth.

What a nightmare. It was like a tug of war: Dad on one end of the rope and Mum on the other, both pulling to see who would fall over first. Well, between Mama Tiny and me, maybe even Janeese, although she's got enough problems with her parents, I wonder if we could somehow get them back together again, I thought. I know that Mum still loves Dad (so what is she doing with this Ian bloke?). Now, does Dad love Mum? How to find out?

I was busy getting myself ready to go out with Dad when he rang up to say that he was going to be about an hour late. That was all right, I could take a bit longer doing myself up. I had taken special care with my hair, spraying some moisturising oil sheen conditioner on it, pulling up the front into a pony-tail and tying a big red ribbon in it. I twirled around in front of the mirror and it was amazing, I really looked like Whitney Houston with braids. To cheer myself up while I was waiting for Dad I put MJ's 'PYT' on (Pretty Young Thing – for those living in the dark ages). 'Honestly, Michael, your voice knows all the hidden parts of me. Like when you hit those high notes, all my nerves tingle and I just can't keep still.' I threw my hands in the air, did a double spin, blew a kiss to Michael on the wall (I haven't played that LP for a long time) and danced round the room. His eyes were so bright, they were following me everywhere, he was obviously enjoying my dancing. 'Stiff competition, eh?' I laughed. I knew deep down that regardless of what anyone said about him, he was the Number One thing on the music scene. I could tell by the way he was eyeing me up that he thought I was a good dancer. 'You should have had me in your 'Thriller' video, I would have been much better than that stupid Ola Rae. Where did you get her from, eh? I could tell from the video that she wasn't a very clever girl and was overcome with being so close to you so she couldn't concentrate on what she was supposed to be doing, and she was really immature. She was so unnatural.' I turned the LP over and put on 'Thriller'. I closed my eyes and went through the beginning of the video, as they sat in the pictures eating popcorn. Then they came outside and MJ started to dance around her (but this time it was really me). I started to walk across my bedroom, giggling as MJ danced around me. He stopped in front of me singing . . .

'Kiesha, yu fadda come. Yu ready?' shouted Mama Tiny.

Her voice made me jump. It's a shock to come back to reality when you are having such a good time.

'I'm coming, Mama Tiny.' I put my shoes on and straightened out my clothes, grabbed my bag and dashed out of the room.

'Bye, Mum,' I shouted out. I knew she would be in her room. 'Bye Mama Tiny.' I kissed her cheek as she stood by the open front door.

I ran out of the house, eager to see Dad. Just as I reached the car door, I felt like someone had put brakes on me. There in front, perched up like a vulture, was Marlene. Dad was busy looking at himself in the mirror. She turned to me and smiled sweetly, then opened the door and climbed out to let me in. 'Hi, Kiesha,' she drooled. I just couldn't speak. What's she doing here? I thought, and how dare she talk to me so familiarly? I screwed up my eyes as though I had the power to make her vanish, but obviously I didn't have it, because she was still standing there all confident, like Tina Turner. I climbed in the back. I should be sitting in the front, he's *my* Dad and this is *our* day out, I wanted to tell her. As the car pulled off, I turned around just in time to see Mum drawing back the curtain. She'd obviously seen Miss T in the front. This would justify her going out with Ian tonight. I could just see the gap between them widening. Right, number three plan to be activated, which was hit dad where it hurt. Number one plan was to break it to him gently about Mum and Ian, number two was to make him jealous and get him to agree to take Mum out and try and get round her but, due to the situation (which I hadn't foreseen), there was no alternative but number three!

'Hello, darling. No kiss for your poor old dad then?' He looked in his mirror at me.

'Where are you dropping Marlene off, Dad?' I asked, ignoring his question. He tried to look back at me, but he had to keep his eyes on the road.

'What's all this hostility about, young lady?' he threw over his shoulder.

I looked out of the window. I was trying to pick my words carefully, as I didn't want to really upset him, but I couldn't see me giving him an easy time – I was preparing myself for war!

'Well?' he asked.

'Dad, I want to talk to you about something quite serious,' I said quietly, trying to create an atmosphere of calmness.

'Well, my booolooloops, I'm sure nothing you're going to say will shock Marlene, she's an old friend,' he grinned.

I knew he was grinning, because his ears moved. How could Dad do this to me? After all the planning I had been doing with Oliver, how could I have overlooked this?

'Kiesha,' Dad said sweetly, much too sweetly for my liking. Trying to butter me up, I know. I just won't answer him.

He coughed. 'Er, I thought it would be nice if Marlene spent the day with us.'

I was stunned. What a mean trick.

'But Dad, Marlene can spend Monday, Tuesday, Wednesday, Thursday, Friday and Sunday with you. I only have a few hours on Saturdays,' I said to the back of Marlene's head, so that she could feel on the back of her neck the venom coming out of my breath. She didn't flinch; obviously thick-skinned.

'To tell you the truth, sweetheart, I thought it would be nice if we all three of us spent the day together just getting to know each other.'

'Dad, I don't want to be rude, but I don't need to spend the day getting to know you and that only leaves one person, whom I don't particularly want to get to know.' There. I said it.

Marlene turned round to look at me. She tried to soften her eyes at me, the way she must do with Dad, but I'm not Dad. I just cut my eye at her, the way I've seen Aunt Audrey do to people. She smiled. I think she's blind, can't she see I don't like her? The feeling is growing by the minute!

'Kiesha, I'm sure we could be friends, if only you tried to relax, honey,' she split the red mass on her face which was her lips, to reveal pearly white capped teeth. The synthetic mass of weave-on on her head looked like a bird's nest – it was very tempting. Pity I didn't have a box of matches! At least that would have been one way of getting rid of her. I suddenly felt guilty. How could I be so horrible to Marlene, even if she was trying to make herself the next Mrs Lyndon Ferell? When I got home, I was going to have to discuss this issue with Oliver and MJ to get some feedback. But wait a minute, if she becomes the next Mrs Ferell, that would make her my step-mum. Right, we'll see about that.

Dad drove around for a while, going nowhere in particular. Marlene said she would like to go to the park. I wasn't even asked. I could see this woman meant business with my dad, so I would have to be very clever. We walked through the park gates, Dad and Miss T. in front, me at the back. The way she was walking was making me feel sick. She was wearing a tight red dress, and her rear was moving around. She had on four-inch high-heeled shoes that made her leg muscles really stand out. She was hanging on to Dad's arm, like it was her rightful place. How Dad could walk along with her looking like a right mess in broad daylight, I just don't know. If only I could get close enough to her, perhaps I could trip her up, I was working it all out in my brain. But then, if she fell over she would take Dad with her and I didn't want that. I just wanted him to see that really, he was making a big mistake with her. I trailed behind them like a little lost lamb. Hmm, she reminds me of a tiger on two legs. Well, baby, it's me and you to the kill!

We sat on the park bench, Dad in between me and Miss T (I really think that name suits her). They seemed totally oblivious of me. I closed my eyes and leaned against the bench. The drone of her voice was enough to put you to sleep, she was so boring. How could Dad laugh? He must've really changed since he met her, and for the worse! Mum was the only person who could make Dad laugh; he wasn't the sort of person that would laugh at any joke and Mum knew just the right ones to tell him. That's why I didn't understand him being with Miss T.

I couldn't figure it out. I just let my mind float away, with the cool wind, her voice, Dad's laughter . . .

Ferell. FBI secret undercover agent. 'Your mission is to destroy secret undercover agent of the KGB, code name Miss T. Don't be fooled by her dumbness, or pretty looks: she's a trained agent, a merciless killer. You've got to strike first, otherwise you could wind up dead. Got it?'

'Yessir.' I stood to attention, in the Boss's office. I was proud to have been called to carry out such a dangerous mission. I straightened up and put my hands behind my back. I was bursting with pride. I couldn't wait to tell Mama Tiny and Mum.

'Ferell, this is Top Secret. You're to tell no one until the job is done, understand?'

'Yessir.' Drat, I won't be able to tell them. Never mind, when the job's done I'll be a national hero.

Standing in the park behind the trees, I pulled out Miss T's photo. I looked up at the woman sitting on the same bench as a very handsome man and really good-looking kid. 'Yeah, that's her all right. Well, baby, your chips are cooked, you've had it.'

I began to assemble my bow and arrow (the FBI allow you to use whatever weapon you think is suitable for the job). A bow and arrow was swift and safe – no sound, no mess, straight to the point of contact, POW! I raised the bow, pulled the arrow back, ready to fire, and let go . . .

'Kiesha, wake up,' said Dad, gently tugging my arm.

I threw myself into his arms. 'Oh, Dad, I'm so glad

she's . . .'

'Oh, you're awake, Kiesha,' smiled Miss T.

I felt depressed. If only my dream were true.

We must have been in every shoe shop in London, trying to get Miss T a pair of shoes. She had such funny-shaped feet, she needed to see a chiropodist to get them sorted out. I bet if I'd wanted a pair of shoes I would have had to settle for a pair in the very first shop!

It was getting late and as we were already in the West End Miss T thought it would be a good idea to eat out. We found an Italian restaurant. I felt a bit rejected. After all, I was an only child and I was supposed to be the apple of my dad's eye, and to have to share my only day with him with a flammable-headed, false-teethed man-snatcher such as she was proving to be extremely unbearable.

Dad and I had lasagna, she ordered spaghetti. As she twisted her fork around the spaghetti and raised the forkful to her mouth, I wished that it would turn into little worms, just as she closed her mouth over the fork. I laughed to myself. The spaghetti fell down her dress and Dad quickly leaned over to dab at it with his napkin. She giggled. She would, I thought. Now was the time to tell him about Mum, just as his mouth was full of pasta.

'Dad.'

'Hmm?' He couldn't speak.

'Mum's going out with her boyfriend Ian tonight. They're going to the theatre around here somewhere,' I waved my arm about for more impact, 'and then I think he's booked up at a plush restaurant to take Mum. She's so excited. She bought a completely new outfit and she's lost loads of weight to get into it. It's a skin-tight sequinned number, she looks like Diana Ross. Ian's so lucky to get Mum.'

I wondered if any of the restaurant staff had taken lessons in first aid, particularly the kiss of life, because from the noise Dad was making it might be crucial to his survival. Miss T punched him in the back.

'Oh Lyndon, what's wrong darling?' She was panicking.

I stood up and tried to get one of the waiters' attention. One looked over and I pointed at Dad. He rushed over and began to beat Dad viciously on the back.

'What is the problem, sir?'

Dad took a gulp of air and waved the waiter off. He couldn't speak. His eyes were protruding out of their sockets and he had spittle running down his chin. I knew he hated to look untidy so he must feel awful. I was overcome with remorse. Why did things have to be this way? I would've really liked it to be Mum sitting here with Dad instead of *her* – I could hardly bring myself to even look at her.

Miss T was petting Dad like he was a domestic cat. I could see her now for what she was, a schemer. But I wanted her to know that she had met her match in *me*!

I touched Dad's arm and said, 'You all right, Dad?' I was concerned. He looked at me and tried to grin. 'Yeah babe,' he said, as calmly as possible, but I felt sure that he still had some lasagna stuck down his throat.

'What happened, Dad?' I asked innocently, my eyes taking on a 'pure as the lily' glaze.

He took a sip of water to push down the remaining pasta and after a deep breath, he was nearly back to normal. 'Er, I think I must've taken too large a mouthful and it went down the wrong hole. Never mind, I'm okay now.' He smiled at me a bit strangely but he couldn't pin anything on me. I smiled back.

'You okay, Lyndon, you feel all right?' Miss T cooed, just like a homing pigeon. Little did she know I was going to disturb her nest.

'Mmm, this pasta is fantastic, we'll have to come here again, Dad,' I said between mouthfuls of food.

He seemed to have lost his appetite. 'Yeah, it's lovely. We must come again.'

Miss T had to join in every conversation, whether it concerned her or not. 'Yes, you're right, Kiesha, it's lovely food. We'll definitely have to book a table and come again.' She screwed up her eyes at me as though we were of one mind. I looked down at my plate. I couldn't stand looking at her, it put me off my food.

I wondered how someone else in a similar situation would handle it. I just didn't know which way to turn. Mum with Ian, Dad with Marlene. I wished this wasn't happening. I was frightened that they might never get back together again. What would I do? How would I feel? I didn't know how to bring this up in conversation with anyone, not even Mama Tiny. It was really winding me up. There must be a way round all this.

Dad seemed to be preoccupied for the rest of the meal. When the profiteroles were served up he refused them, so I ate them. Mmm, delicious. It might turn out all right after all.

We left the restaurant as soon as we had drunk our coffee. It was still quite light outside, the cool evening summer air just what I needed to lift my spirits. I felt good inside, perhaps because of the delicious food (it certainly wasn't from having Miss T around), but if I'm honest with myself, I was happy that what I had said about Mum and Ian had got up Dad's nose, or rather, in his case, down his throat!

As we walked to the car, Miss T held on to Dad's arm as though she was frightened he would run away from her. Good sign.

'Lyndon, what shall we do now?' she squeaked. I had noticed throughout the evening that whenever she was sending out her silky threads to entrap Dad, she put on this voice. I could see she was using all her weapons. While I was trying to figure out what to say in response, Dad got in before me and I must say it took me by surprise.

'Marlene, I think it's time I took you home.' He smiled at her, revealing his perfect set of teeth with the gold-capped one at the side. I knew for a fact (having experienced it myself) that once you saw that gold tooth flashing away at you – move! But Miss T did not know the sign.

'But Lyndon, you said that . . .'

He stopped just before the car. 'Look Marlene, I said I'm taking you home and that's that,' he said softly.

It was clear she didn't have much brain (what little she did have must've been packed into that tight dress): 'But darling . . .'

Dad's face turned to stone. Bad sign. What I had said about Mum must've affected him very badly. Good.

'Ma-r-le-ne,' he drawled between clenched teeth, 'you are go-i-ng h-o-m-e. Get it?' He walked around to the driver's door, opened it and got in, then leaned across and opened the passenger door. I climbed in and Marlene wriggled herself in the front seat. Well, I thought, I have to give her ten out of ten for trying.

'Listen Lyndon, what's the problem, have I said something to upset you?' she asked.

No, I thought, it's something *I've* said. I sat in the back and snuggled down into my seat. Watching Miss T and Dad was like watching TV: *Dynasty* had nothing on what was happening here.

'Listen Marlene, it's nothing you've done or said, I'm not angry with you or anything, but I just feel that it's time I took you home. Okay? I'll ring you tomorrow or some other time.' The car pulled forward and we were away.

'Lyndon.' She turned around to face him as much as the seat belt would allow, 'I think we need to talk' – she looked at me – 'alone.' Desperation was written on her face. Bye bye Miss T, so much for your song: 'Let's Stay Together'.

Dad didn't seem to hear her, he was miles away. Mind you, the way he was driving we were all miles away, fast.

'Hmm,' was all she got for her efforts.

We drove along in silence. I knew Dad was going to question me, so I was trying to work out the right answers to make it sound good, without making Mum appear to be neglecting me, because Dad might try to use that line – he had done it before.

'You can drop me home, Lyndon,' whispered Miss T.

Oh, what a shame. I did feel a bit sorry for her – after all she was quite innocent in all of this, but after watching programmes like *Dallas* with all the wheeling and dealing, you realise only the strong and wicked survive! I was feeling proud of myself, especially now that I felt sorry for Marlene (I'll call her by her proper name), which meant I was human after all.

He pulled up outside a private block of flats. Dad didn't even turn the engine off. Marlene undid her seat belt and turned to Dad – with tears in her eyes. I felt sick. Oh, I'm really wicked, I thought. I wanted to tell her not to worry, but the words got stuck in my throat. Then she said, 'Lyndon, I love you,' in a really soft whisper, but I heard her. Oh, that slippery cat. In front of me, his daughter, she was willing to let herself sink so low. Well, if this is what love does to you, making you act like you have no shame, I don't think I want it! 'Lyndon, I love you,' I mimicked her in my mind. She was grabbing at straws, anything to hold on to Dad. That was when I stopped feeling sorry for her.

She climbed out of the car, giving Dad little 'sorry girl' looks. As she shut the door, she turned to me in the back seat and if looks could kill . . . Need I say more? I knew what she was up to. I just looked her dead in the eye.

Dad revved the engine and we drove off.

We pulled up outside the door and Dad jumped out and went round the other side to open the door for me. I climbed out slowly, praying that Mum wasn't home yet, or better still that she hadn't gone out. The vibes from Dad said he might be a little mentally unstable at the moment.

He rang the bell.

Mama Tiny shouted out, 'Who is dere?'

'It's Lyndon,' answered Dad.

We could hear the chains rattle and the bolt being drawn back. The door opened and there was Mama Tiny.

'Hello, son, solong mi nar see yu. Yu look good,' she beamed. Dad smiled; I kept my eyes down.

'Come in, come in,' beckoned Mama Tiny.

Dad stepped straight in as though he was used to the house, while I slipped in, trying to escape upstairs.

'Kiesha, yu not goin to seh goodbye to yur fadda, chile? Whe yur manners dere?' asked Mama Tiny.

'Oh, I'm sorry Dad, I wanted to go to the loo.' I turned and walked over to him, kissing him on the cheek. 'It was a lovely day, Dad, thanks.' I smiled a special smile-for-dad.

'I wanted to speak to you, Kiesha, but we can leave it for another time.' He just looked at me.

I flew up the stairs. When I got to the top I heard Mama Tiny say that Mum was out.

I went straight into my bedroom and down on my knees. The time for messing about was over, this situation called for some crucial, divine help! I prayed: 'Dear God – forgive me for being a little wicked to Miss, oops sorry, Marlene, but as you can see I'm only trying to see if I can get my parents back together. I know you want us to be a family as much as I do, so I'll be needing your help. Firstly, please don't let Dad wait for Mum to come home, let him come back another day when he's calmer. I hope I'm not overtaxing your resources by asking you this favour. Thanks a lot. Amen. Er, in case you don't know my name, it's Kiesha, and I will make an effort to go to church more often.'

I jumped up off my knees and began to pace the room. I walked up and down so much I must've done about ten miles! I was really sweating. I heard the front door bang. My heart missed a beat.

'Kiesha, come down,' shouted Mama Tiny.

You know, Mama Tiny has a powerful voice for someone her age and it can frighten the life out of you.

'Kiesha! Did yu hear me chile?' she bellowed.

I thought I had better send up one last prayer, it might be my last! 'Dear God, protect me from danger, namely Mama Tiny. Amen.'

I took my time going downstairs, trying to think of positive answers that were definitely going to be needed for the difficult questions I was going to be asked. I didn't want to lie – only if I had to!

I walked into the living room. No sign of Dad. Thank God.

'Hi, Mama Tiny,' I said as brightly as I could. She wasn't fooled.

'Siddung.' She looked at me sternly. 'What yu bin talkin to yur fadda, ee?' she quizzed.

I was relieved. Dad was definitely not here and Mum hadn't come home yet – good, it gave me time to think.

'What do you mean, Mama Tiny?' I said innocently. It was better if Mama Tiny told me her side of the story first, that way I would know what angle to come from.

'Yu tell yur fadda dat yur madda gwan out wid Ian, an bout she dress up favour poppy-show. Chile, what do yu ee, why yu go fas tell yur fadda bout yur madda business ee? Bwoy, oonoo picknee mouti-mouti ee ee.' She kissed her teeth. She folded her arms. Then she leaned towards me, pointing her finger at me, 'Mi nar know what gwine happen now, it look like pure murderation. Picknee, it come in like you ave goat mout, cha.' She kissed her teeth again. I was glued to my seat. Mama Tiny had the ability to tell you everything and nothing. I wondered what Dad

97

had told her.

We sat in silence. I couldn't speak, because Mama Tiny would say that I'd said enough and would probably tell me to shut up. So I said nothing. We sat like that for a while.

Mama Tiny couldn't keep silent for long, so she just came out and asked me what I had told my dad. So I told her what had happened from beginning to end. The amazing thing was, Mama Tiny started to laugh.

'Serve yur fadda right. Him an yur madda still love one anudda, and dem shoulda never part inna de first place, cha.' She kissed her teeth. 'Well, Kiesha, what ever yu did sey, really upset yur fadda.' She grinned at me and her top denture nearly fell out.

I was pleased with myself. Mama Tiny wasn't upset, but Dad was. Things looked good.

'Mama Tiny, can I wait up for Mum to come back?'

'Okay darlin, gwine put on yur nightie an mi will mek some Milo fi drink, yu see.'

I floated up the stairs, feeling on top of the world. Whoopee!

We sat in the front room chatting about what had happened. I was very tired though.

'What time is it please, Mama Tiny?' I yawned.

'Hmm, two o'clock. Yur madda a stay out late, ee?' she yawned back.

We must've dozed off, because the next thing I knew Mum was shaking me to wake up.

'Why haven't you both gone to bed? You shouldn't have stayed up for me.' She smiled into my face, stroking my cheek. I looked up, a little hazily at first, and then broke into a smile and threw my arms around her neck.

'Okay, okay darling, I'm so glad you're pleased to see me,' she laughed. I looked over at Mama Tiny, who wasn't smiling, and I was just going to ask her what was wrong, when Mum said, 'Well, ladies, you might as well meet Ian. I invited him in for a night drink.'

I looked up and (I'm sure he was at least eight foot tall) there was Ian. He had a bushy beard and when he took off his glasses I knew straight away that he must somehow be related to Lloyd Honeyghan. He looked like his twin with a beard.

'Hello, Kiesha, sorry to have to meet you at this unfortunate hour. I've heard so much about you.' He smiled, revealing an even set of very white teeth.

I didn't move. He was handsome, there was no mistaking that, and had a lot of charm. All I could think was that he was going to be stiff competition – how was I going to get rid of him?

'Oh, I see you're shy. Never mind, we'll have plenty of time to get used to one another.' He grinned, showing his teeth.

It hurt me to smile, but I managed somehow. Oh boy, this is going to be one hard nut to crack!

Nine

Janeese and I were walking very slowly along Ham Park Road on our way to the park. This was the third time this week we had been there. I was glad it was Friday. The Youth Centre was holding a week of sports activities, in the evenings as well as at the weekend. We weren't taking part, it wore me out just watching! The evening was warm and there was no way that I felt like wearing trousers or even a dress, so we had both decided to put on our shorts. We looked wicked! My mum had bought me a pair of those mirror sunglasses. I loved wearing them, because I could stare at people and they didn't even know it! Janeese had treated me to a really sickly sweet ice-cream cornet; it was nice. We were just licking our fingers when a car passed by with three white boys in it shouting out of the window:

'Oi, darling, lovely legs.'

'Nice bit of female stuff.'

'Do you want a lift? C'mon, get in.'

They stopped the car and started to reverse back towards us.

'Pretend we haven't heard them,' I said to Janeese, pulling her arm.

'What's the matter, too good for us are yer?'

'Don't listen,' I hissed.

Janeese laughed. I couldn't see what was so funny.

'C'mon, let's go, I can't be bothered with girls like that.' Voorm, voorm, a screeching of rubber and they were gone. Good.

We both giggled about those stupid boys. What a cheek, expecting to pick up two respectable girls like us. You could tell they were only used to dealing with a certain type of girl!

As we walked alongside park, we could see through the park railings. There was already a crowd of young people and the closer we got, the louder their voices became, a bit like the Notting Hill carnival, without the costumes.

I was really hot. Even talking was hard work and I couldn't stop sweating, it was pouring off me like a water fountain. We walked along in silence. I had to fan myself with my paper tissue, not that it helped much. Thinking about those boys in the car, I wondered what it would be like going out with a white boy. I really couldn't imagine it and wondered how Janeese felt, so I asked her. 'Janeese, would you go out with a white boy?'

She looked a bit thoughtful and bit her lip. 'Hmm, I don't know,' she sighed.

'Honestly, Janeese, anyone would think that it was a million dollar question. You only have to say yes or no.' I had to fan myself because it was so hot.

Janeese twiddled her hair; she reckoned that made her think! She had started to look well trendy now and she had somehow managed to persuade her mum to let her have her hair relaxed – she had it all out loose, nice.

'Well, in that case, yes.'

My feet stuck on the pavement. 'What! What did you say?' I was so shocked.

She just carried on walking as though she had only told me the right time, then said it again, 'Yes.'

I ran to catch up and started talking fifteen to the dozen. 'What do you mean, yes you would go out with a white boy? I can't believe it.'

'Why not? I think they're all right.'

'You think they're all right. What's wrong with black boys, eh? Think of all the really good-looking ones you know and think of all the ones that you don't know and then think again about going out with white boys, I mean, I don't think it's right!'

She turned round to look at me. 'Kiesha, I just think you're being stupid. I don't think looks is really important, right? Okay, it counts a lot at first, but after a while it's not the looks that you have to put up with, it's their attitude and how they treat you and all that sort of stuff.'

'I don't think you know what you're saying. You know what your trouble is, you watch telly too much,' I told her.

Then Janeese, without batting an eyelid, calmly turned round and said, 'Okay, let me put it this way, if you had to choose between Beacon Wallis and a white boy, who would you choose?'

I nearly choked. 'That's' – I took a deep breath – 'that's a situation that would never occur, so therefore it's not worth answering. Anyway, you only want to get out of

101

answering my question sensibly.'

'I have answered sensibly and I've asked you a question which you haven't answered, Kiesha. Now come on, who would you go out with – Beacon Wallis or a white boy?'

I just couldn't answer. I tried to think about it seriously, but it was impossible. The thought of slimy Wallis near me made me want to fetch up my ice-cream. He was awful. 'No, sorry,' I shook my head, 'it's an impossible question, it's unanswerable.' I shrugged my shoulders.

'Well, there you go, there's nothing more to say, except I don't watch too much telly, I don't have to, I just watch my parents and other adults and that's all the education I need. Anyway, I think that sometimes you know what's it all about and then at other times, Kiesha, you seem so childish I don't know what's going on in your head. I think you need to open your eyes a bit more.'

I was ready to come back at her with a piece of my mind, but I couldn't be bothered. You know what, since her brother's party, it was as though Janeese had had a metamorphic change (see, I do study biology – good old Andrew's Liver Salts). She wasn't the quiet girl I first knew, she was like a flower in full bloom and there weren't any bees on her either! Look at her, she had started to wear different clothes (my suggestion) and changed her hairstyle and I had even caught her wriggling her bum (I had to look twice), especially when boys were present. Now all this talk about white boys was a real shocker and then to top it off, she was more or less saying that I'm immature!

This white boy business got me though. You see, in our area only girls who don't care about what anyone says about them go out with white boys, or if they think they are 'something', you know, like a pop star or a model, they might, but mainly everyone sticks to their own. I tried to picture myself with a white boy, but the nearest I could get was George Michael. Now, he's well fit, but you don't see his sort down our way! Anyway, he isn't white white, he's more Mediterranean, and he's hairy, hmm, not bad, not bad, and he's always in the sun. Yeah, he was worth thinking about. Then I thought of Dean Bean (yes, that is his name, poor boy). He isn't bad-looking, he's had his hair streaked and he looks quite presentable. He had been out with at least four black girls, who were all right, you know. I tried to imagine myself introducing him to my dad – he would have a fit, but then even if he was black he would still have a fit! I wondered what my mum would say. Hmm, George Michael, cool mover – I'd rather have him or even Dean Bean than Beacon Wallis any day!

We walked in the gate and made our way to the crowd. Neither of us said a word. I felt a bit let down. Well, when you're close friends with someone, you tend to see certain things in the same way. I was surprised that Janeese said she would go out with a white boy. I looked at her from the corner of my eye. Well, they would have nice kids. Oops, I sounded like Mama Tiny, that's the sort of thing she would say. I felt a little hurt too. Since I had taken Janeese under my wing, she had not walked but run ahead of herself – and me! Now she thought she was as wise as me concerning the matters of the world and, as far as I can see, she can't handle herself – she's just like a little bird who's not quite learned how to fly, so she's still struggling to leave the nest. I felt a little better after thinking that. Now perhaps I could forgive her for calling me immature: she doesn't understand the runnings she's dealing with.

Beacon Wallis called us over. I didn't want to go at first, but then I recognised some of the people that were near him from our school. We walked towards him. Someone had brought a powerful ghetto blaster and I tell you, it was powerful. Some of the boys were breakdancing and a crowd was gathering around them. They were really good. There were some stupid girls throwing Coca-Cola from their cans over a group of boys. I could see them

103

getting their teeth smashed in soon.

You could tell the sports freaks from the onlookers. They all had their sports gear on, mostly designer. They were limbering up, stretching and flexing their bodies, boxing the air and kicking or bouncing balls. The rest of us who were spectators were really just hanging about, talking, making jokes, you know, killing time. Janeese spied her brother Neal somewhere over to our left.

'Hey Kiesha, there's Neal,' she said nudging me. She called out to him and began to walk towards him.

I grabbed her arm. 'Janeese, have you said anything to him about me?'

She stopped and said, 'No. I didn't know what to tell him.'

'Oh no, remember you were going to fix up a time for us to meet together at your house?'

Janeese rolled her eyes up and put her hand on my shoulder. 'Kiesha, I think Neal's a little too old for you and, from what he's been saying, he just sees you as a friend of mine, and to tell you the truth' – she looked at me all concerned – 'I'm not upsetting you, am I?' I shook my head, I couldn't speak. 'I don't think at this time that he would ask you to be his girlfriend.'

She looked me in the eye and squeezed my shoulder. 'Anyway, he's got a horrible temper and in some ways, he's quite like my dad, and if you did become his girlfriend, later on you would probably be against me for not warning you about what he was like.' She smiled and took my hand and we walked over to where Neal and his friends were.

I was choked. The thing was that what Janeese had said was probably true. I seemed to be so 'boy mad' and caught up on looks that I didn't stop to think about what his personality was like. He could be Jack the Ripper's grandson for all I knew! You know, it's really hard to take what someone has told you, especially if it's true and you don't want to hear it. I sensed a cloud of depression hover over my head and I felt cold, even though the sun was out. I wanted to cry and had to bite my lip to stop the tears from flowing. Talk about rejection, how do you deal with it? I felt like I needed a good cry – for losing Neal, even Jamal, about my mum and dad, and Marlene and Ian (I wonder if those two could somehow pair up?), my ex-friend Stacey turning out to be a traitor, Janeese for telling me the truth and showing me how worldly-wise *she* is. After sobbing my heart out I might feel a bit better and then I could have a bit of a dance around my room with MJ!

I wanted to go home.

'Hi, Kiesha,' smiled Neal.

He did look gorgeous, though. He had white shorts and a Fred Perry shirt, white trainers (I bet they cost the earth) and socks, all matching his white teeth.

'Hello, Neal,' I said shyly. I felt that he could see through me and it must've stood out a mile that I fancied him. 'Do you want a drink?' He offered me his can of Coke.

The temptation was too much, he had just had his lips around the can. I really wanted to drink from it.

'No thanks, I've just had an ice-cream.' I smiled back at him. I felt right grown-up being able to refuse something that I wanted. I should try out these new feelings again.

'Hello Janeese, hello Kiesha. What's happening, girls? You both look very, very nice, I must say, in your shorts,' smiled Jamal.

'Hello,' was all I could squeak.

'Hi,' said Janeese.

As usual the two ugly sisters (Stacey Bailey and Streaky Bacon) were hanging on to his tail. They gave me daggers. I just pushed my nose in the air. Nothing better than riff-raff.

Janeese and I found an uninhabited patch of grass. We

sat down and just let the rays of the sun wash over us. The music in the background was loud and beaty and I began to tap my feet to the rhythm. The voices in the background were like when you have the radio on but not properly tuned in and it crackles and hums.

We sat there in silence deep in our own thoughts. Mine were about Janeese (again). Since we had been friends she seemed to have come out of herself. It was as though she had needed a way to get what was inside out and having me as a friend had helped her to do it. I had to admit, she seemed a lot happier now than when I first met her, which I supposed was a good thing. I thought she would turn out to be a better friend in the long run than Stacey Bailey.

I don't know for how long, but the background music had stopped and the voices had got louder. I looked up and found I was the only one sitting down. Even Janeese had got up, why hadn't she called me? What's going on? I stood up and walked towards where a crowd had gathered.

Janeese must've seen me before I saw her. She called me over: 'Kiesha, Kiesha, come here.'

'What's happening?' I grabbed her arm.

'It's Beacon Wallis, he's having an argument with some boys I've never seen before.'

Beacon Wallis along with Neal and Jamal and Brent Collins and some other boys I didn't know were standing in a kind of circle, while we formed another circle outside them.

'Listen guy, you can't come round here, right, and carry on like so, right?' said Beacon, all flash.

'Yeah? So what you gonna do about it, eh?' said a boy I'd never seen before.

'Right, you wanna know, do yer?' said Beacon.

'No, Beacon, leave the guy alone. Can't you see he's just a kid?' said Jamal.

'He wants me to waste him,' Beacon said, leaning his

head to one side.

This is stupid, I thought, none of it makes any sense. Beacon, just mouthing off as usual. No big deal. Anyway, that other boy looks as though he can handle himself. Let's hope Beacon's physical is as bad as his mouth!

Neal got in between Beacon and the boy. 'Hey, listen, right?' he said to the boy. 'We're cool this side, you know, so why don't you just back off, right, and just let the games go on, right?'

Well, actually the games *were* going on, it was only us lot really that were not involved in them.

The boy stepped closer to Beacon. 'Gonna waste me, c'mon then.'

The next thing I saw was the boy falling backwards. I couldn't believe it. Beacon must've really whacked him one. There was a bundle on the grass.

I turned to Janeese: 'I don't want to watch this. Come on, let's go.'

'No. I'm staying. I'll only go if Neal goes.'

'I just don't believe this. What's special about watching stupid boys fight? Oh, look, forget it, Janeese. I'll see you later.'

I pushed my way out of the crowd and walked towards the park gates. Turning back to look, I saw a couple of Youth Centre workers running towards the crowd. I thought that Janeese might have followed me, but she was too concerned about her brother. So what about me? I couldn't believe that some people could enjoy watching others fight. Well, I hope that Beacon got his jaw broken. I bet he started the fight anyway, with his big mouth.

I decided to walk the long way home. I crossed the road and saw two policemen looking towards the park. I hoped they would go in and perhaps Beacon would get arrested. 'Yeah, serve him right,' I said to myself.

I thought about Janeese. First saying she would go out with a white boy and now leaving me to go home alone, more concerned about her brother than me. I mean, he's a big boy and can take care of himself, what was she worried about? She should think about herself, and me!

Mama Tiny was coming down the stairs as I let myself in.

'Chile, what do yu ee?' she asked.

'Nothing,' I said.

She kissed her teeth. 'Mi ask yu a question, well?'

'Well, it's everything really. I'm just a bit fed up.'

'I don't know how yu ave time fi fed up when yu coulda read yur Bible,' said Mama Tiny, pursing her lips.

The front door opened and Mum came in. 'Hello Mama Tiny and Kiesha.' She looked at me a bit closer. 'What's wrong with you, why the long face?'

'Same ting mi just ask her, a young gal like dat.' Mama Tiny kissed her teeth again.

'I'm going to my room if anyone wants me,' I said, taking the steps two at a time.

Even though it was still quite early, I got ready for bed and snuggled cosily under the quilt. I looked into the mirror of the dressing-table, which reflected the picture of MJ on the wall above my bed. I thought he looked bored, so I started making faces at him. He didn't laugh, so I stopped. I didn't feel tired at first, but next thing I knew I was nodding off. It seemed that no sooner had I fallen asleep than I was dreaming that I was floating in the air with all the clouds around me. I wasn't frightened or anything, I felt light and airy. I bounced gently into clouds and sometimes I found myself right in the middle of one and the cotton-woolly stuff that clouds are made of tickled me and got up my nose and made me sneeze. It was great fun, I was having such a laugh. The sun was on my back, but its rays couldn't burn me because the friendly clouds stopped them from penetrating.

'This is great – no worries, no cares, no one to bother me, no need for anyone else, just me, hurrah!' I said to the clouds. I was having a ball. I didn't mind that I was on my own, the less people around the less trouble there would be.

No sooner were those words out of my mouth than lo and behold, there was a policeman. I don't know where he had come from. He had stripes all down both arms, which told me he must've been high up in the police force, and he had the biggest baton I have ever seen in my life in his hand, waving it around in the air. It was nearly as big as him and he was at least nine foot! Fear and panic seized me. Where could I run to? I began to look around for somehwere to hide. Nowhere. I could sense that something bad was going to happen. The policeman started to come towards me. I began to cry.

'What's wrong, little girl?' he smiled, but it was a smile that spelt DANGER. I tried to back away from him, but bumped into a cloud that bounced me back towards the policeman. He made a lunge for me and I screamed 'Leave me alone, leave me alone.' Just as he grabbed at my arm I felt myself falling, down, down, down. It all happened in a matter of seconds.

Landing with a bump on some grass, I looked around, taking stock of the place. To my left I could see a pond with ducks on it and to my right children were playing on swings. I sighed with relief, it was a park. I had successfully got away from that horrible policeman. I was sitting on the grass, trying to gather my thoughts together on what to do next, when I heard a terrible thud beside me. 'Oh, no, it's you again,' I wailed, and scrambled to my feet. It was the policeman. He had fallen out of the sky.

'Er, thought you got away, didn't you? Well, I'm going to get you now!' He made a grab for me. (I sent up a quick prayer as I knew that God was watching all this, and it must've been in answer to my prayer that for the moment I managed to escape the clutches of the evil policeman.) I ran across the park as quickly as my legs would carry me, with the policeman in hot pursuit.

I reached the edge of the pond and couldn't decide what to do next, but before I knew it the policeman had caught hold of my jumper and his arm was hooked under my neck.

'I've got you now, little black girl. I'm going to eat you for my supper.' He turned around and carried me off, where I don't know, but by the sound of it I'd only be having salt, pepper and water for company, when he put me in his pot. I managed to find my voice box and, with a rush of air from my lungs, I bawled out at the top of my voice 'HELP!'

The policeman laughed. 'Ha, ha, there's no one to rescue you.'

'HELP!' I went on shouting, not giving up.

We were halfway across the park, when I caught sight of a magnificent black horse, with a very imposing rider, riding towards us. As he passed, he managed to snatch me from the policeman's grasp and rode off at full speed, faster than the wind. I hugged the horseman so tight, saying 'My hero, my hero.'

He put one arm around my waist and gave it a squeeze. 'You are my princess and I am your prince,' he said. I smiled.

The horseman lifted back his helmet and, as I turned to reward him with a kiss, I froze – it was none other than Beacon Wallis! 'Oh, no,' I screamed, 'from the frying-pan to the microwave.' I struggled and fought with Beacon Wallis to let me go, but he only laughed. 'I've got you now, you're all mine. Ha, ha.' The horse began to gallop like crazy while Beacon and I were wrestling.

'Let me go, you evil boy.'

'I have you now, you belong to me, ha, ha.'

'Help, help . . .'

Mum was standing over me, pinning my shoulders to the bed.

'Kiesha, Kiesha, it's okay darling, you're safe now, it's all right.'

'What? What? Oh, Mum.' I threw my arms around her neck and sobbed. 'Oh, Mum, it was a horrible dream.'

She sat on the side of my bed and held me in her arms. 'What was it about, darling?'

'Oh, Mum, it was a horrible dream. I dreamt that a policeman was after me and he was going to cook me in his pot and then I was rescued by Beacon Wallis and he wouldn't let me go. I was caught between two evils, it was horrible.'

'Hush now, Kiesha. You're letting the bad dream get to you, eh?' She kissed me. 'Beacon Wallis isn't that bad, surely, though I'm not too sure about the policeman.'

'I prefer the policeman any day to Beacon.' I yawned.

'Anyway, how come you're in bed so early? If I had sent you, you would've kicked up such a stink. What's wrong? Don't you feel well?'

I rubbed my eyes. 'Yeah, I'm okay. It's just that, well, everything is going wrong.'

'Like what?'

'Well, it's Janeese. You know what happened over the park, Mum? Stupid Beacon Wallis got himself into a fight. I said to Janeese that we had better go home and she said no, she wanted to stay with her brother. But Mum, he's seventeen years old! I couldn't believe it. She didn't care whether or not I got home all right, to look after her older brother.'

Mum laughed. 'Oh, Kiesha, I don't blame her. Blood is thicker than water, you know. She probably wanted to stay to make sure he was all right, I don't think she was looking after him. That's what brothers and sisters are for, to look out for one another. Stanley and Tim and I and the others used to do it all the time. In fact we do it now, though obviously we don't get into fights now.' She smiled.

111

'Well, I wouldn't know about that, I have to fend for myself.'

'Now, now. A bit touchy, aren't we? We all know that Kiesha Ferell is an only child, but we won't hold it against her.' Mum looked down at me. 'But you're still my baby and I can see that underneath all that "big woman" chat there's still quite a bit of my little girl, eh?' she said.

'I think I'm very grown up,' I said, sitting up a bit.

'So now that you wear a bra, you're a woman I suppose?'

'Not only that, other things,' I said.

'Oh well, I'll be expecting you to be bringing home your wage packet soon, in that case.' She laughed.

'I don't think that's too far off, so you won't be laughing when I do.'

'Oh, Kiesha, what am I going to do with you?' she said.

'Can I go skiing next year with the school?' I thought I'd get that one in.

Ten

The morning sun burned through my flower-patterned cotton curtains, its rays washing over my body like healing ointment. I woke up feeling a bit depressed about what happened yesterday with Janeese. Not even the sun, which usually cheers me up, could help this time. I tried to sit up in bed, but I just didn't have the energy and after all the rest I'd had, I should have been able to run a hundred metres in two seconds! I could hear Mum and Mama Tiny talking downstairs. I wondered what happened to Janeese and the others.

I thought about Janeese telling me yesterday that she would go out with a white boy – I just don't understand her. Then I remembered what she had said about her brother going out with me. It was probably true, she's not the sort of person to lie over something like that – what had she got to gain if she did? It's funny, you know, people the world over always seem to fall into the same trap. How a person dresses, or what car they drive, or where they live, or how good-looking they are, or how much money they have are what attract people to each other. The list could go on and on. I can't say that I don't go by those things – I'm just as bad. I had liked the look of Jamal, without thinking what he was like. I had made excuses about him having Stacey and Streaky Bacon hanging around him, when really you can tell a person by the friends they keep (that's what Mum says) and I feel that this is good, sound advice at times, but I don't think you can say that it's always true.

Dad was working in Birmingham this weekend, I had no plans to do anything in particular. I didn't want to go downstairs and then again I didn't want to stay in bed. I didn't know what to do with myself. I stretched across the bed for Oliver and gave him a cuddle, he needed it. I kissed his nose. I looked up at MJ's picture. 'Oh, Michael,' I whispered to him, 'you don't have any trouble at all. You have a great career, all the women you want (including me), all the money in the world, no problems.' He smiled back at me as if to confirm what I had said. 'Some people have all the luck.'

I put my hands behind my head and began to think over everything that I could remember about yesterday.

I wondered if Beacon Wallis got it in the neck – it would serve him right, his mouth was too big. I hoped that Neal hadn't got involved, fighting could spoil his good looks. Anyway, with a sister like Janeese 'looking out' for him he should be all right! I snuggled down under the bedclothes.

I wondered if I could become a recluse. Well, I don't see why not, all the rich people do; when they've earned too much money and don't want to give any away, they keep away from people. Let me see, that would mean no school, no wandering around the high street shopping with Mum, good. No church, although I'd miss the music. I thought about going out with Dad and parties and shopping for clothes. Hmm, I don't think I'll be a complete recluse, maybe I'd be better off as a semi one! I smiled to myself, yeah, that's better.

I got up and drew the curtains. The flowers in the garden were being gently blown by the cool morning breeze. 'I think I'll go and see Janeese today, I don't think she's doing anything special,' I said to myself, looking through the window. I began to sort through my wardrobe for what to put on. Hmm, I wonder if I should walk to Janeese's house.

When I got downstairs Mum was hoovering the hall. 'Morning, Mum.'

'Morning, Kiesha. Glad to see that a good night's sleep has done you good.'

'Oh, Mum. I must be better looking for it, after all, it was my beauty sleep.'

Mum laughed. 'You're a nut case. Go on, go and get something to eat.'

'Morning, Mama Tiny.' I breezed into the kitchen.

'Marnin, chile. Waan yur breakfast now?' she asked.

'Yes please.'

Mama Tiny put a bowlful of cornmeal porridge in front of me. I suddenly didn't fancy anything to eat and pushed it away.

'No thanks, Mama Tiny.'

'What happen, chile, it too sweet?'

'No, I just don't want it,' I said, turning up my nose.

'Yu don't know how lucky yu is, picknee from all over de world wou.' just nyam up de sinting, quick time.

114

Come yu mus eat it,' she said, pushing the bowl back to me.

I sighed. What a drag. I had a spoonful and just stirred the porridge in the bowl to make it look as though I had tried. Honestly, Mama Tiny thinks I'm a baby. There wasn't any point saying anything, she would probably go on and on.

I got up from the table and said, 'I've finished, Mama Tiny,' making a quick exit so that she couldn't collar me.

'Mum, is it all right if I go to Janeese's house?'

She turned the Hoover off. 'Okay, for a little while. Don't be too long now.'

As I was about to knock on Janeese's door it opened.

'I saw you coming up the road,' she smiled.

'I was going to phone you, but I didn't think you were doing anything today, so I thought I'd just come round.'

'That's all right. Come in.'

We went into the front room. It was a bit overcrowded with furniture, the two two-seater settees taking up a lot of room. There was quite a big record collection in the corner, LPs stacked on top of one another. 'Whose are those, Janeese?' I pointed to them.

'Oh, my dad's. His favourite is Paul Robeson.'

'Who? I've never heard of him,' I said.

'He's really got a deep voice. He's good, though,' Janeese said.

The telly was under the window, with the video underneath it. At the side were loads of video tapes.

'Who watches all those?' I asked.

'Who do you think? Neal. He's a video freak.'

I sat on a settee. 'Well, how did yesterday go?'

She shrugged her shoulders. 'All right, I suppose.'

'What happened to Beacon?'

'Oh, Beacon, he's really a good fighter, you know. He gave the boy a good going over.'

115

'Who? Beacon Wallis? I don't believe it. He's such a creep. What about Neal, did he get involved?'

'Well, yes and no, he was sort of a referee. Funny enough Jamal got his finger broken,' she said.

'Did he? Was he fighting too?'

'Not that I could see, but that's what Neal said.'

We sat quietly for a moment and then I just had to ask her. 'Janeese, do you still think that you would say yes to going out with a white boy?'

'Oh, Kiesha, you're not still going on about that, are you?' She leaned back against the settee, folded her arms and closed her eyes. 'Kiesha,' she said, sounding a bit fed up. 'People are forever going to pick on other people for one thing or another. If it's not colour, it's religion, or because you're poor or you're a woman. The story of people trying to keep other people down will always be going on and on. Do you know, in the West Indies, the lighter skinned you are the better job prospects and marriage ties and the best of everything you get. If your hair is straight and your features are too, well, you've no problem getting anything you want.'

'That's not true, Janeese, and you know it and if those things did ever happen it's only because the slave owners kept telling us that's how life goes, after they made all the women pregnant. Anyway, you're only saying that to get out of answering truthfully and that . . .'

Janeese sat up. 'No, I'm not. Okay then, perhaps I would have to seriously think about having a white boyfriend, but what I said about the West Indies is true. In America it's the same, even in this country,' she pointed to the floor. 'Listen, even white people, who started this discrimination thing off, discriminate against each other, Irish, French. Look at the Second World War, it was mainly white people killing off each other. They're mad people and even us blacks are beginning to pick up their bad ways.'

116

'It's only because they drummed it into us in the first place, I keep telling you,' I mumbled.

I was getting really mad. I wanted to shake Janeese and call her a traitor and all sorts of names. My fists were clenched and I could feel the anger inside. I felt a hand on my shoulder – it was Janeese.

'Kiesha, I know you're angry, we all get like that over these things. I'm just about fed up with this fighting over colour, when will it end? That's why I said that I would go out with a white boy, just to be defiant. My dad hates white people. I can understand, he has been through a lot with them and it wasn't good stuff. My mum tries to talk to him about his hatred and he goes mad. We near enough have it in our house twenty-four hours a day. We don't talk to our neighbours for that reason. It wasn't Dad's fault, they started it, and I don't know who's right and who's wrong. But Kiesha, I don't want to live like that, hating people all my life, because the thing about hating people – and I've seen it with my dad – is that it starts to affect you and destroys you. That's one of the major reasons our family is splitting up, because of hate.'

'What – hating white people?'

'No, not just that, but my dad, it seems, hates everyone who doesn't agree with him, and he can never see that perhaps he might be wrong. But the funny thing is it's the men in this situation who don't talk to one another, but the women do. It's crazy.'

'Well, I know I hate policemen.'

'Well, yeah, that's a different thing altogether. You know, I think if women had all the jobs that men have the world would be a better place. How about mainly women policemen? Ohh, that sounds really funny, women police-men, ha, ha.'

'Yeah, what about women firemen?'

'No, no, Kiesha, what about women gasmen?' laughed Janeese.

117

We were both laughing now. 'Janeese, Janeese, what about a woman Prime Minister?'

We both stopped laughing, 'What about one?' she said, looking at me from the side of her eyes.

'Oh, I forgot. Well, she's like a man anyway. I mean, women who are women.' I grinned.

'Okay, how about Kiesha Tashana Ferell for Prime Minister?' shouted Janeese.

'Hurrah, long live Kiesha, hurrah for me!'

We both rolled about on the settee laughing.

'Oh, Kiesha, you'll always be my friend, won't you?'

I sensed the pleading in her voice. 'Oh course, wild horses wouldn't drag me away from you. Listen, when we leave school we can share a flat together, and when we get married we can live next door to one another.'

'Yeah, that'll be great.'

'Janeese, how many children do you want?' I asked her.

'Hmm, this many.' She held up ten fingers.

'Oh no, you're joking, how are you going to feed them all?'

She laughed. 'I'm going to marry a manager of a supermarket and we'll get our food cheap.'

'Why don't you be a bit more ambitious and marry someone who owns a supermarket?'

'Yeah, that's a good idea, but,' she said, eyeing me, 'what if he's a West Indian Indian?' She smiled.

'A West Indian Indian, what's that?' I screwed up my eyes. 'Hmm, I'd have to think about that one.'

Janeese jumped up and started searching the drawers of the cabinet in the corner of the room. She came back to the settee with a photo album. 'Guess who this woman is.'

She handed me a photo of an Indian woman whose long hair trailed down her back, outside a beautiful detached house surrounded by trees and flowers. It looked hot wherever she was.

'I don't know, who is she?'

118

'She's my grandmother, that's who she is.'

I held the photo up closer to my eyes to get a really good look. 'She looks like your mum. Look at her hair, she looks like an Indian lady. Her skin is right dark and all.'

'There we go back to colour again. In Trinidad, there are so many different races living side by side, every one is mixed up. I think that the world over will soon be like that, I mean, it's becoming that way now. Then who will hate who? We'll all be related to each other.'

'Yeah, then we'll really have fun. Even in the same family people don't get on.'

'Yeah, don't I know it,' said Janeese.

Just then the door opened and Neal walked in with a big grin on his face. 'Hi, Kiesha, how are you?' he smiled.

'Oh, Neal,' I said rather breathlessly, I couldn't help myself. 'How are you?' I said, looking right pleased to see him. Well I was, wasn't I?

He came and sat down between us. 'I'm fine, just a bit tired, that's all. Too many late nights, I suppose.' He leaned back on the settee.

'How about everyone else? You know, Jamal.'

'Jamal's broken his finger trying to protect Stacey and Gail, who were holding on to him. He had his arm around them and somehow or other his finger got broken. It was amazing, you know, the way Beacon took on this guy. He's really strong, he was going crazy, punching and kicking. His face got cut up a bit, but he really battered this guy.'

I was only half listening, thinking about Jamal. Serves him right. I screwed up my mouth and eyes. Getting his finger broken protecting those two. 'I wonder if he would have done it for me,' I said under my breath.

'What's that Kiesha?' asked Neal.

'Oh, oh nothing,' I said. I was glad he couldn't read my thoughts, otherwise he might think I was a wicked person, and I wouldn't want him to think that, would I? But then

119

how was I supposed to feel when my boyfriend went off with my ex-best friend and then, in defending her, got his finger broken? It's not nice, is it?

Then I remembered what Janeese had said about Neal not fancying me – could she have got it wrong? Here was I sitting a goosepimple away from him and he didn't even know how I felt. Janeese is probably right, he just sees me as her friend, a little schoolgirl!

'Kiesha,' Neal said, putting his arm round my shoulder (I'll tell you what, if I wasn't sitting down I would have fallen down!), 'I got really worried when we couldn't find you. What happened to you, eh?'

'I just felt like going home, so I did. Sorry if I caused you any worry.' I smiled up at him.

'That's all right. As long as you got home safely.'

He hugged me. I nearly melted away. I snuggled closer to him. I wondered if Janeese could've got it wrong about me and Neal after all. The way he was going I was just waiting for him to ask me out!

'Kiesha,' he said softly. (I thought he was going to pop the question any minute now and that he was speaking softly: (1) for special effect and (2) because he didn't want Janeese to hear what he was saying.)

Ooooohhh . . .

'I er, I was really worried about you yesterday, ask Janeese.' He turned to her: 'Wasn't I, wondering where she had got to?'

'Yeah, it's true, Kiesha. Neal was getting a bit worried about where you were,' she said.

I had shivers going up and down my spine, the hairs on my arms were standing up, waiting for what Neal was going to say.

'You know,' he said, all husky, like Lenny Henry taking off Alexander O'Neal, 'you've become sort of special to me and I would like to keep it that way, okay?' He smiled at me. I looked at Neal and it was as though all my dreams

120

were coming true. I half closed my eyes dreamily waiting for his next move.

'Yeah,' he squeezed my shoulder, 'you're like having another little sister around.' He put his other arm around Janeese. 'Yeah, you're like twins, you go so well together. Kiesha,' he turned to me, 'just think of me as your older brother. Anything you want, or someone needs sorting out, just look me up, okay?' He tweaked my chin.

The phone rang. He got up to answer it: 'That'll be Tasha, seeing if I'm all right. That girl really loves to worry about me, I don't know.' He went out of the door.

Air inside me dwindled down to nothing and I felt faint. I wanted to cry out that it was unfair, and the thought of him regarding me as a little sister made me want to cry even more. I bit my lip. I sensed that Janeese could see that I was very upset.

I was trying to contain myself, but I couldn't. 'Who's this Tasha? She sounds like a cat,' I said, blinking my eyes rapidly to stop the tears.

'It's his girlfriend, or should I say one of many? He changes them so quickly it's hard to keep up with him.'

A big lump came into my throat, making it hard for me to breathe let alone talk. 'Er, hmm, his girlfriend,' I squeaked. I was devastated. I felt such a fool for letting my heart run away with itself. How could I be so stupid? Of course, a boy his age and looking so good is bound to have a girlfriend. Funnily enough, that thought cheered me up a bit. He obviously didn't realise that I liked him. If he knew, perhaps he might ask me out. But I knew that he meant it when he said that he saw me as his little sister. What a loss!

Janeese moved closer to me and leaned forward, looking right into my face. 'I tried to tell you, Kiesha, but I didn't know how to put it about Tasha. I really didn't realise how much you thought about Neal. You're upset, aren't you?'

'Well, yeah, I suppose so. Nothing's gone right for me for the past couple of weeks,' I sighed.

Janeese put her arm around my shoulder and I put mine around her. We sat there for a while, just hugging each other. I felt so close to her at that moment, she was really like how I imagined a sister would be. It made me realise how selfish I had been. I was forever thinking about myself, my happiness. I found myself feeling really guilty. 'Oh, Janeese, I'm sorry to have to put you through all this, I should have listened to you in the first place. I don't know if I really loved Neal, it was just that he was nice looking and he was so nice to me, I thought that he might really like me.' I felt like crying and squeezed her tighter.

'He really likes you, but as he said, like a sister.'

We separated and leaned back into the softness of the settee, smiling as best we could at each other.

'You know what, Janeese, it's true what Neal said about us being like sisters. You're closer to me than Patrice and Renita, you've taken the time to get to know me.'

'And you've taken the trouble to get to know me. I think that's what's wrong with people in this world, they don't get to know each other properly. Take my mum and dad for instance, I don't think they know each other at all – how they got married I don't know. Mum said that Dad seemed to be more interested in her looks, and she just liked the attention, and when he kept telling her how much he loved her, that did it, they got married. She said since they've been married, he hasn't once proved it to her! They could've saved themselves all this trouble if they had found out what each other was like. It's so stupid,' she sighed.

'C'mon, let's go out for a walk up the high street,' I said.

'I have to get dressed first,' Janeese said.

'Oh, Janeese, who cares? You don't look that bad.'

'You sure I look all right? Okay then, c'mon.' She got up.

Janeese really surprised me. To think that before I met her, her clothes were outdated, but now she was up the front for fashion!

We walked up the road, arms linked. The sun had come out and it just felt nice to be strolling along with your best friend. Anyway, I was glad I hadn't got a boyfriend, they just seemed like a lot of trouble.

We walked past the shops, looking in the windows at things we couldn't afford to buy. We went into Young Thing boutique and tried on all the clothes, mixing and matching them. As we came out, we bumped into Beacon Wallis. I was shocked. His face looked as though someone had used it as a football. It was odd-shaped, swollen and covered in bruises, with one eye closed up. In short, he looked terrible.

'Beacon, oh, no! Look at you,' said Janeese, all concerned.

He tried to grin his stupid grin, but somehow it just never came across. He lifted his hand and said 'Hi,' then put it in his pocket and shuffled his feet and looked down, as though he was embarrassed. I can honestly say that it was then that I realised that Beacon Wallis was a human being. Now, I know that may sound awful, but before, he was always taking the mickey out of people, joking about, like a fool, you just couldn't take him seriously. I mean, he wasn't stupid, stupid, he did have a brain – in fact he was very good in maths, I wouldn't have believed it myself if I wasn't in the same class. I'd hardly seen him with a girl, putting it down to the fact that most girls in their right mind wouldn't go out with him. But, according to Neal, quite a lot of girls did fancy Beacon! I suppose he must know: when all the boys get together they all talk about us girls. I didn't believe it at first, but he assured me that Beacon had a way with girls. Never, I thought, he's too much of a creep. But there you go. Looking at him all battered and bruised I did feel a rush of guilt touch my heart. (Rather poetic I thought, that last bit!) He looked like a little stray waif.

'You all right, Beacon?' I said softly. I did mean it.

He squared up his shoulders in true macho style. 'Yeah, I'm fine, what about you?'

'How do you find me?' I grinned a bit stupidly, I don't know what came over me.

He looked at me with the eye that was swollen and, kind of turning to one side, put his hand on his hip. Talking out of the side of his mouth and with an American accent, he said, 'Yeah babe, you look fine from where I'm standing. Come up and see me some time.' He tried to grin.

Janeese and I thought the same thing, we discovered when we talked about it later. I mean, here he was, been through the wars and he was still trying to pose and impress! Would you believe it? We started to laugh and it wasn't long before Beacon joined in.

'Hey, what's the joke?' he said.

Janeese and I both said together, 'You', and laughed all the more.

He stopped laughing. 'Yeah, I'm glad I can make you laugh. HA, HA.' He turned to walk off.

Janeese grabbed his arm, but he pulled away from her, with 'You're just a bunch of silly girls, anyway.'

Now as I've said previously I don't know what was happening to me, usually I would never be seen dead laughing with Beacon Wallis and after he was so rude to Janeese and me, I would have given him a mouthful of verbal that would have burst his eardrums.

Instead, I said, 'Please don't go, Beacon.' I even held out my hand to him.

He stopped. I could see that he was eyeing us both up, to see if we were genuine in what we were saying. 'Okay,' he mumbled. He could see we were for real.

'Shall we go to McDonald's?' Janeese asked, looking at Beacon and me. We looked at one another, shrugged our shoulders and agreed to go.

On the way Beacon cracked some hard jokes that had Janeese and me in stitches.

When we got to McDonald's Beacon said, 'Okay girls, this is my treat. What do you want?' Janeese and I were lost for words. You see, we had heard that Beacon Wallis was tightfisted: he would never spend his money. Girls that had been out with him (they must've been head cases) usually ended up paying for him!

We both said that we wanted a Fillet O Fish and chips, apple pie and a large strawberry milk shake. Get in while the going's good, I thought.

'Okay girls, find a seat and I'll get the food.' He swaggered off to queue up.

Janeese and I found a window table and sat down.

We both giggled. This was really funny. I would never have imagined in a million years that I would be eating in McDonald's with Beacon Wallis and him treating me. I could see Janeese's mind working overtime. We looked at each other and burst out laughing.

'Oh, Janeese, what do you reckon?' I said, stuffing my fingers in my mouth to stop myself laughing.

'I don't know, what do you reckon?' she laughed.

As Beacon came towards us with the tray of food Janeese whispered to me,' I think he fancies you rotten,' and put her fingers to her lips.'

'Oh, thank you, Beacon.' She smiled up at him. He grinned and looked over to me. I was still trying to get over what Janeese had said and offered him a watery grin. We all sat there grinning.

'Well, get into the food, ladies, otherwise it'll get cold,' said Beacon, all mannish.

I didn't feel hungry any more. Janeese and Beacon were tucking into their food as though eating had just come into

125

fashion, but I was right off mine. What if it were true and Beacon did fancy me? Well, I sure didn't fancy him. I knew that for certain! I picked gingerly at the food. With my stomach all queasy I didn't want to force anything down it.

After we had finished, or rather after they had finished, Beacon pulled a packet of cigarettes from his pocket. 'Want one, girls?' he offered.

'No thanks,' we both said together. 'In fact I'm allergic to smoke,' I added. He's so stupid smoking. I know he's only showing off, idiot! I could feel my old sarcastic feelings towards Beacon coming out and, to tell you the truth, I just didn't care. Well, that's not true, it's not that I didn't care, in fact I truthfully didn't know how I felt about anything any more.

You see, when I looked back to even a few weeks before, and then thought about what Janeese said about Beacon fancying me, I had a funny feeling that it might be true. I remembered the night of Neal's party and all those things that he had said about me over the microphone, and to think that I had thought it was Jamal! Beacon was just like the weather: the sun could be out, the day nice, but a couple of hours later, rain. That was him spot on – nice weather until he came along!

As far as I could see Beacon and I had never really got on, but (and it's a big but) Mama Tiny told me about the time when Grandfather and she were courting. They didn't like each other at first and Grandfather used to get on her nerves. But when she saw him with another woman Mama Tiny said she didn't know what came over her (she said it was probably jealousy), she literally threw herself in Grandfather's path (I can't imagine Mama Tiny doing such a thing). Anyway, it turned out that the 'other' woman was a cousin of Grandfather's. So it worked itself out in the end. Well, I've seen Beacon with some other girls on and off (he didn't know I was taking any notice of him) and all I felt was sorry for them. No feelings of jealousy had a home in me, or any other feelings for that matter. I wondered if Janeese was just saying that. Mind you, I do recall that she had mentioned it before. Hmm, I'll have to wait until afterwards to speak to her about this.

As we were leaving the McDonald's Beacon said to us, 'What are you doing now, girls?'

We looked at each other.

'Nothing,' Janeese said.

'Going home,' I said.

'Well, I've got a good idea. I bought some new records the other day, you can come round to my house and listen to them if you like.' He grinned.

That stupid boy was beginning to get on my nerves.

'Thanks for the offer, but I've got to go home.' I smiled tightly. Why does he want us to go home with him? I thought. Who knows what he's going to do to us, I know for a fact he's not all there! Anyway, for all we know, he could live in a squat or somewhere revolting. I don't want to be too friendly with him.

I couldn't believe my ears when I heard Janeese say, 'Yeah, that would be great, wouldn't it, Kiesha?' She looked at me.

Well, if eyes could talk she, by right, would be knocked out! I really didn't want to be rude to Janeese in front of Beacon but she was making it very hard for me to be otherwise. I didn't want to go to his house, couldn't she see?

'Well, hmm, I'm quite busy at home and I've got to go now.' I grinned, showing all my teeth.

Now, as far as I could see, this fantastic 'sister' relationship that Janeese and I were supposed to have was rapidly becoming a thing of the past.

'C'mon, Kiesha, you haven't got anything to do at home,' said Janeese, folding her arms.

'Look girls, there's no need to argue. I would really like

127

you to come home with me, only for an hour or so, and you can phone your parents from there and tell them where you are, but, if you really don't want to come, I understand, you know, you have to be in early and all that.' He looked from me to Janeese.

It was only about four o'clock and I knew that Beacon was being funny, but like a fool I rose to the bait.

'I'm sure I can spare a little time at your house, Beacon, and as for the time,' I said in my Lady Di voice, giving a little laugh to show him I didn't care, 'I have all the time in the world.' What a big mouth.

Beacon and Janeese walked along the high street chatting and laughing. I could have not been there for all they cared. Beacon was mimicking people along the street and Janeese was killing herself laughing. I couldn't see what was so funny – my face was a mask of stone! We had to cross the road, so we stood on the kerb – and Beacon held our hands. I nearly died. Who does he think we are, his children?

'Hey, what do you think you're doing?' I grabbed my hand away from his.

'Look, I'm just making sure we get across the road in one piece, but please yourself.' He let go of my hand and crossed the road with Janeese. I was only a moment behind them when a car bore down on me as though it was trying to kill me – and would have, if I hadn't darted across to the other side of the road. It scared the life out of me.

Janeese rushed over to me: 'Are you all right?'

'No, I'm all left.' I tried very hard to smile as though everything was fine and that it was no big thing being nearly killed by a mad driver. Beacon never said a word, he just looked at me. If he was waiting for me to say something, he'd be collecting his pension before I would.

We carried on walking past the last few shops, which included the steak house. It's really expensive in there, I know, because Dad took Mum as a treat quite a few times.

Just then Beacon opens his big mouth and says, 'I'll take you both in there one day,' all flash like.

'Oh, really,' I said to him, 'after you've done overtime on your paper round.' Janeese laughed. I was glad I had said that, I felt like my old self at long last.

Beacon said to me,' No, I have money, you know. I could take you in there tonight, but you have to be home, so perhaps some other time,' and carried on walking.

What a big-headed creep. I could feel something rising up inside me, which was just waiting for Beacon to say the wrong word at the wrong time and BANG, was he going to get it in the neck!

I was just level with the steak house (the other two were ahead of me), when this couple came out arm in arm and I froze. My mouth dropped open and my eyes nearly fell on the floor. I couldn't believe who it was – none other than Miss T with some bloke. We-ell! Of all the cheek. There she was doing the Juliet bit, hoping my Dad would be her Romeo, and all the time she was stringing him along, double-timing him. I looked her square in the eye. She put her head down and tried to walk past me. The man with her smiled at me.

I said 'Hello,' and he grinned at me but Miss T kept her head down. 'Hello, Marlene,' I said sweetly. She ignored me. The man stopped, looked from Marlene to me and then from me to Marlene.

He said to Marlene: 'Do you know this young lady?'

She sort of smiled and said, 'Er, not much. Come on, Colin, we're gonna be late.'

But Colin (I knew his name now) turned to me and said, 'How do you know Marlene?'

The moment I'd been waiting for. I took a deep breath and said very quickly, 'Marlene is my dad's, Lyndon Ferell that is, girlfriend, of course, and I met her the other day, because we all went out to dinner.' I smiled, revealing my teeth and gums.

'I don't know what you're talking about,' she said, with a flash silk scarf round her neck and her finger on her chin (pity it wasn't a noose round her neck).

'You must remember, it was an Italian restaurant and Dad nearly choked on his lasagna, and when we dropped you off you told Dad you loved him.' I beamed. This was great, I felt good.

Colin (I was getting to like him by the minute) said, 'Thanks a lot, love. I'm glad I met you. Thanks for the information,' and smiled, really cool like.

'Come, you,' he said to Miss T, grabbing her under the elbow and marching her off.

I felt so good I could have floated. I ran up to the others, wanting to shout out at the top of my voice. When I told them what had happened Janeese asked me if I was sure that I had done the right thing. 'Of course,' I said. Beacon just looked at me. I wasn't looking for his approval anyway.

When we got to the top of Beacon's road I didn't believe he lived there. It was all posh-looking. It was very quiet, and the houses, most with front gardens, were enormous, with sleek-looking cars outside! Beacon's house was beautiful. In the street there was a tree heavy with new leaves whose branches hung over Beacon's front garden. He opened the door with his key, so I thought that he must live here. As soon as I stepped inside it felt cosy. You know some houses have that kind of feel to them as soon as you enter them. He said it was a four-bedroom house and he lived here with his elder brother Neville, his mum and his grandfather.

'Beacon?' said this woman's voice. Must be his mum, I thought.

'Yes, Mum,' he shouted back. I was right.

Into the hallway came this very attractive woman, really sophisticated – not false like Aunt Audrey, but like she had got everything together. She looked young too and reminded me a little of my mum. I wondered if they were the same age.

He introduced us and we shook hands. She said that we had better phone our parents to say where we were, and would we like something to eat? We told her we had just eaten at McDonald's. I phoned Mum, who said it was all right to stay for a little while but to come home soon.

Beacon took us up to the spare room. I wasn't too sure I wanted to go. Why couldn't we stay downstairs with his mum? I still didn't trust him. When we got into the spare room I could see why: it was decked out like a recording studio. Along the walls and in every corner was a machine of some sort. I could pick out a tape recorder, by the big spools. I remember my dad having something like that. Half the length of one wall, from floor to ceiling, were records.

'Boy, this must be really worth a lot of money, Beacon,' I said. It took my breath away seeing all this equipment and records. I was impressed. Janeese was wandering around, touching everything.

'Like it, girls?' He grinned. I could see that he was in his element.

I wanted to say I didn't like a thing, but I couldn't: 'Yeah, it's nice.'

Beacon produced an electric guitar from somewhere, plugged it in and started to play it. It brought back memories of church. He was strumming out some chords and then he started to make up words to go with them:

> I ain't got no money
> But I love you honey

He looked at me and smiled. I smiled back. Janeese and I caught each other's eye and even though she didn't say it, I knew that she would've said that he was singing for me.

131

He sang some more:

> You'll be my f-l-y girl
> And I'll be your h-o-u-s-e boy

Janeese and I started to laugh. Beacon glanced at us, smiled and then closed his eyes and really got into his guitar. He started to stroke it like a cat and it responded. The guitar seemed to become part of him, as though it was stuck on his body, and the way he moved around, it looked as if he was trying to shake it off. He twisted and turned, his arm sometimes moving quickly across the strings, then slowing down, and it made your insides light up just to look at him.

Someone came in. I knew because I could sense a presence near me. Turning round, I saw it was Beacon's grandfather and mouthed hello. Janeese did the same.

By now Beacon was sweating. He raised one leg as he was playing and threw back his head, really getting carried away. It was so stimulating, I could've watched him all night. He began to slow down, then stopped and opened his eyes, which held a dreamy, faraway look. His grandfather clapped, so we did too – he deserved it anyway, he was very good. Well, I could see Beacon in a new light now.

His grandfather said, 'Bwoy, yu ave talent, ee?' and grinned and patted his head. He turned to look at me and said, 'Mi know yu face from somewhere, ee?' He frowned.

I smiled and said, 'From church.'

His face lit up. 'Oh, is yu an yur grannie mi di drop ome. Tell her howdi do for mi, see. She is a gracious lady.' He grinned a bit too enthusiastically. 'Yes, she's a fine strappin ooman.'

I didn't like the way he said that. He didn't fancy Mama Tiny, did he? He's too old. I soon sobered up with that thought, not that I was drunk, mind you. Well, not on booze, but maybe on music.

I looked at my watch and then at Janeese. 'I think we should be going now,' I said.

'Yeah, I think so too,' said Janeese.

'Thanks, Beacon, that was really nice. I never knew you could play the guitar so well,' I said.

'There's a lot you don't know about me, Kiesha.' He grinned.

Can't he do something other than grin?

'Oh, really?' I grinned. Oh boy, it must be catching.

We made our way downstairs. His mum met us at the bottom.

'Going now, girls? It was nice having you. Did Beacon treat you nice?' We nodded. 'Dad, would you mind taking these ladies home for me, please? That way I know they'll be getting home safely.'

In the car Beacon's grandfather chatted and chatted about how Mama Tiny reminded him of someone he knew and what a 'fit ooman' she was. He was getting on my nerves and, of course, I couldn't say anything. Now I knew where Beacon got it all from!

They dropped me off at the house and waited until I opened the door with my key.

The last thing Beacon said to me was that he would ring me. It wasn't until I was upstairs in my room talking to Oliver about the day's events (I couldn't talk it over with MJ, as I knew only too well of his deep feelings of jealousy), that I wondered where he had got my phone number from.

Eleven

The smell of curry was making me very hungry. It's funny, you know, how you don't feel very hungry until you catch a whiff of something appetising which starts your gastric juices off (Mr Andrews' biology was always cropping up in my thoughts) and you feel as though you could eat anything.

I felt comfortable lounging in Dad's reclining armchair. I looked around the room, which he had decorated tastefully, or rather, he paid someone to decorate it for him. Dad said he preferred other people who were professionals to do certain things for him, like decoration, so that a good job was done. Mum said that Dad was lazy.

I tipped the chair back a little and gazed up at the ceiling. He had had it Artexed with a shell-like pattern all over it and painted cream. Hmm, quite nice. He had an expensive-looking lampshade, which he claimed had cost him the earth. Mum had said he could afford it.

I ran my hands over the leather of the chair: it was cool and smooth, just like my dad. Dad's three-piece suite was leather too, and black. The carpet was cream and so were the walls. His bookcase was stained black, as was the low wooden table in the centre of the room. I bet that Marlene felt she had hit the jackpot when she walked into the flat, after she had got over the car, of course!

Over the meal that he had cooked (it made a change from eating out) Dad kept asking me polite questions about Janeese and how I was getting on at school. I knew that he wasn't particularly interested, what he really

134

wanted was some info on Mum. Well, he had better ask me because I wasn't going to volunteer anything.

Here we go. 'How's your mum these days?' said Dad, sipping his lager.

'Oh, she's fine, just fine.' I nodded.

'How's her diet going?'

'Diet? What diet?' I asked innocently.

'I thought you said that your mum had lost weight, that she had been dieting.'

'Oh no, she just seems to be busy these days, going to the theatre quite a bit. I suppose that helps her to keep her weight down.'

Dad kept his eyes on his plate. 'Must be that new friend of her's that's keeping her busy.'

I knew that Dad still felt 'something' for Mum. Why didn't he just come out and say it? If he didn't I could see that I was going to.

'If I remember rightly she didn't like the theatre, how come she can't stop going now?'

I looked him in the face, 'It's probably Ian that's taking her there.'

'Who's this? The new boyfriend?'

'I suppose so.' I looked down at my plate. I didn't like the way Dad said that.

We carried on eating. I watched Dad. He was tucking into his meal as though he didn't have a care in the world.

'Dad.' He looked up. 'Do you love Mum still?' I whispered.

He put his fork down and wiped his fingers on his napkin. 'Does it matter?'

I shrugged my shoulders, pretending not to care.

'Okay, for your sake, yes, but that doesn't mean that we're going to get back together again, well, not for now anyway. All right, you happy now? I don't want to talk about it any more.'

I couldn't finish my meal. I wasn't sure if that was the

135

answer I wanted, but he did say that he still loved Mum, which was a good sign.

We were sitting relaxing, Dad in the armchair, me in the reclining chair, talking about nothing in particular, when the phone rang. Dad spoke for a minute or so and then took the rest of the call in the bedroom. I tipped myself back in the chair going over what he had said. Not bad for an evening's work, I thought. Then I thought back to the day I caught Marlene coming out of the steak house with Colin. When I had got home from Beacon's house that evening Mum wasn't home. Mama Tiny wanted to know who had dropped me off and I told her about Beacon's grandfather being so nosy and calling her a 'strappin ooman'. I expected her to explode, but instead, she laughed her head off. It's funny when people behave completely opposite to what you expect them to. I thought Mama Tiny was going to rant and rave, but laugh – well, you live and you learn. She had wanted to know everything Beacon's grandfather, 'Brother Wallis', had said about her. Hmm, strange that. I wondered what she had up her sleeve.

Then I told Mama Tiny about seeing Marlene coming out of a restaurant hanging on some man's arm and that his name was Colin, and they looked like they both knew each other very well. I wanted to phone Dad straight away, but Mama Tiny said no. At first it upset me because I thought telling Dad about Marlene right away would get her out of the way. But Mama Tiny had other plans.

'Listen chile, if yu get ole a de blade, mine how yu draw it,' she said softly, pointing her finger at me. Mama Tiny speaking in riddles always intrigues me, but this time I didn't know what she was on about and felt it was really uncalled for: this was a time for action.

'Mama Tiny, what do you mean?' I sighed.

'Well chile, yu ave to be very cartious in dis situation. Yu ave fi tink bout what yu gwan tell yur fadda an when.

Yu ave fi work pon im so dat when yu lick im wid what yu know, it will shock up im brain.' She grinned at me as I knew what she was talking about.

'Yeah, yeah, I see what you're saying, Mama Tiny, but what do you suggest that I do?' At first, I didn't know what she meant when she tried to explain what she thought I should do, but gradually, as she told me in more detail what was what, I could see what she was getting at.

Dad came into the front room. 'You okay, honey?' he smiled. 'I'm going to wash up, do you want a drink?'

'No thanks, Dad, I'm all right.'

'You sure?'

'Yeah, fine.'

After doing the washing up, Dad took me home.

In the car, I thought back to the last time Dad had taken me out. It was funny how it all fell into place. You see, Marlene wasn't sure whether or not I would tell Dad (she must've been either very stupid – which she was – or very brazen). I had gone through rehearsals with Mama Tiny about how I was to drop the bomb if (1) Dad was on his own or (2) Marlene was there. I didn't think that Marlene would be there the next time that Dad came for me, but she was.

Okay Miss T. You're gonna be blown out today!

She suggested to Dad that we go to the new West Indian restaurant that had opened up recently in West London. When she first saw me she smiled at me as though I had kept her secret. Well, she was in for a big shock. I prayed about the situation and I'll tell you what, God must've really been in on it, because it worked out better than I could ever have imagined.

In the restaurant, Miss T was queening it over me and drooling over Dad.

'Lyndon, you look so handsome tonight.' She pouted. Dad smiled at her like a twit. (But then, I'm beginning to

137

understand that men love to be flattered even if they know that you are lying. Fools!)

We were halfway through the meal when I saw three men come in and sit down not too far away from our table. Only I could see them, as Dad and Miss T had their backs to the door. One of the men, who was sitting practically facing me, looked familiar. I kept thinking, who is this man, I know I've seen him somewhere before, but where? He caught me looking at him once or twice and I quickly buried my head into my plate.

Dad asked me what was wrong. 'Oh, nothing, Dad.' I smiled back at him.

Miss T kept smiling at me, as though we were bonded together in a top secret.

I know exactly when it hit me. My first mouthful of sweet-potato cake was sliding down my throat when I realised where I had seen this man before: it was with Miss T coming out of the steak house. Now was the time to drop the bomb. But first, I looked over at Colin, our eyes met and we both smiled. Little did he know that he was going to be involved in a melodrama that would outdo any episode of *EastEnders*!

'Er, Marlene, was that your boyfriend you were coming out of the steak house with the other day?' I smiled a special smile for her. She looked up from her plate a bit quick. I must have caught her off her guard. She looked at my Dad and then back at me. She was lost for words, I had put her on the spot.

I did at that moment feel a little sorry for her, but then, I wanted my parents back together again, so I had to be ruthless.

'What are you talking about Kiesha? When was this?' She tried to look unworried but I could see through her.

'You know what I mean, Marlene, that man whose arm you were draped over, last Saturday. I just assumed,' I said in my Lady Di voice for special effect, 'that Colin, I think he said his name was, was your boyfriend.'

Dad raised his head and said very softly, which I knew was a danger signal, 'What are you talking about, Kiesha?' He didn't smile.

I launched into a lengthy explanation about seeing Marlène coming out of the steak house, in the high street, with 'some man'. I kept being interrupted by Marlene, who eventually came right out and called me a liar. Oh, the evil in her voice was deadly!

Dad looked at me, then at her and back at me, and said, 'Are you sure, Kiesha? It could have been someone else.'

'No Dad, I spoke to her,' I insisted.

'It wasn't me, Kiesha. Why are you telling lies on me?' She started to cry.

Dad reached out and touched my arm: 'Let's leave it, shall we? You and I can talk about it another time, Kiesha.' He went back to his meal, but I could see that he had been disturbed by what I had said. I was a bit angry too: if I had said something about Mum having a new boyfriend or something like that he would have got mad. He wasn't too happy about Ian as it was.

'I'm just going to the loo, Dad. I won't be long.' I got up from the table.

Marlene, through her tear-stained face, looked at me with a half-smile on her face. I smiled back. I went over to the table where Colin was sitting and whispered in his ear. His face went rigid. He got up from his table as I was making my way to the loo and I didn't dare look back.

The loos were quite plush. They smelt nice and clean. Nobody was about. I examined my face in the mirror which went right along the wall above the sinks. I washed my hands. I didn't know what to do with myself. I went into the middle loo (there were about five of them), pulled down the lid and sat down. Well, I thought I would be in here for a little while so I might as well make myself comfortable. I rested my elbows on my knees, cupped my

139

face in my hands and I tried not to think about what could be happening outside.

I closed my eyes and the weirdest thing happened. I heard chains clinking and looked up to see a crowd of rough-looking boys, dressed in chains and leather gear, really hard, standing in the loo with me. Then they parted and who do you think sprang out of the middle of them? My very own MJ, singing:

> Your butt is mine
> Gonna tell you right

I looked down at myself and somehow I had on my black woollen tube skirt and black T-shirt. MJ stretched out his hand and pulled me up and we started to dance, while the crowd of boys around clapped. It was great.

> Because I'm bad, I'm bad –
> you know it

Everyone joined in with the singing. It was out of this world – I couldn't believe that it was really happening to me. I was really glad that I had taped the '*BAD*' video because I knew all the movements. MJ just stood back and let me take the floor, and when I did my double spin, all the guys including MJ started to clap and whistle:

'C'mon baby, move yer body.'

'Get to it, sugar.'

'That's right, honey.'

But what really did it for me – and made me do the splits and jump back up again – was when MJ clapped and everything stopped and he said, 'Cool off fellas, the girl is mine.'

He looked to me, his eyes all moist, oozing love and kindness just for me. 'Oh, Michael.' We stood still and just drank deeply from each other's eyes.

'Kiesha, I want you to be in my next video. I want you to be in my life – always.' Then he spun round and shouted out: 'I'M BAD.'

He held my face in his hands (he said I had soft skin) and leaned towards me, pursing his lips to kiss me. I closed my eyes . . .

'Is your name Kiesha?' said a woman, banging on the door of the loo. 'Are you all right in there?'

I stood up shakily, 'Yeah, yeah,' and unlocked the door.

'There's someone waiting outside for you. You sure you're all right?' she said. I nodded.

I walked out of the loo in a daydream. I was a bit stiff too – sitting in that position for so long had made my joints seize up and what with all that dancing, I needed a rest!

I saw Dad standing by the till, looking a bit ruffled. My eyes scanned the restaurant for any sign of Miss T or Colin, but they must've gone home. Hurrah. I tried to suppress a smile. As I drew nearer to Dad I could see that he wasn't happy.

'Where have you been, young lady?' he said, a bit sharpish.

'I was in the toilet, Dad.' I looked at him innocently.

'Doing what? I've been waiting out here for ages for you.' He put his hand in his pocket. 'Come on, let's go.'

I followed him, dying to know what had happened, but I didn't think it was the right time to ask.

We drove in silence until we got to my front door. Dad turned the engine off. We both sat deep in our thoughts.

'Dad, what's wrong?' There. I said it. I could've bitten my tongue.

He turned to me and patted my head, as thought I was a six-year-old.

'Kiesha,' he sighed, and then ran his hand over his eyes. 'Oh, it's just some women. They're more trouble than they're worth.'

141

'What you mean, Dad, is that Marlene was more trouble than she's worth. Look how she lied about being with that man and it was all true, and you didn't believe me, Dad. I was really hurt about that.'

'So, you knew that Colin was in the restaurant, eh?' Oh no, I thought, me and my big mouth. 'I, er, I only recognised him just as I was going to the loo, and he sort of smiled at me and I . . .'

'Okay, Kiesha, that's enough. I suppose you wanted to prove a point and anyway, I don't want to get mixed up with women who are like that.' Dad leaned his head back against the car seat and closed his eyes.

'Anyway,' I said, 'that Marlene was well crustie. Look how much grief she caused you, Dad.'

Dad looked over at me and said, 'What do you mean by crustie?'

I had to think at first. 'Well, seeing how she can be messing about with two men at the same time – that's crustie.' I nodded.

Dad laughed. 'That's a new one on me. Well, I suppose that in this case she fits the bill.'

A picture of Mama Tiny came into my head. I could just imagine what she would say to this situation: 'No everyting dat ave sugar sweet. Yu tink sey smaddy is one way, but yu find seh dem is anudda.' Then she would fold her arms and purse her lips.

I began to think what Mum would say about the evening. She would throw a fit to know that Dad had got me mixed up with his girlfriend and another man! I knew she'd been holding off telling me about my dad and what he was like. I was beginning to find out.

'It's getting so bad these days, it's becoming hard to find a decent woman. All of them seem to be out for what they can get. It's terrible,' Dad said, rubbing his eyes.

'Not all women are like that, Dad. Mum certainly isn't,' I said.

142

'Your mother is a different case, but at the end of the day she is still a woman. Anyway, I'm glad that you're my daughter and it's been nice watching you grow up into a young lady, and so far I haven't seen any of your mother in you.' He smiled.

He turned the key in the ignition and fired the engine. I knew that meant that I had been dismissed, but I didn't get out of the car because I couldn't believe what I had just heard. How could Dad think like that about women – and about Mum! I would be very happy to be like Mum when I get to her age, and to think that Dad had just lumped all women into the same boat – with Marlene! I was a bit angry at Dad, something I have never felt before, and I just knew that I had to say something before I got out of the car.

I undid my seat belt and turned right around to face him. 'Dad, I just can't believe what you said. How can you put Mum in the same group as Marlene? Mum has never done anything like what Marlene has done to you, yet you sound as though she has. It's not fair to judge all women the same. I bet Mum doesn't think that all men are the same. I mean, just look at Marlene, the way she dressed and carried on, it was disgusting. Mum's not like that, nor is Aunt Audrey, nor Auntie Susie, and definitely not Mama Tiny,' I shouted.

'Hold on, Kiesha, you don't understand what has happened . . .'

'But Dad, I do. I'm wondering if *you* understand.' I was really angry now.

'Look, love, I don't think it's the right time to be talking like this. Let's leave it for another time, eh.'

I felt that Dad had copped out. I didn't think there was anything else to say.

'Bye, Dad,' pecked him on the cheek and got out.

'Bye, honey. See you next week.' He drove off.

★

The bright moon lit up the sky. The air was warm and still. I pulled back the bedclothes and breathed deeply. I had not been able to sleep properly for most of the night. I leaned across the bed and turned on the bedside lamp, flooding the room with light. I sat up, propping the pillows behind me, and put Oliver on my lap.

'Well, now let me see.' I began to think about what had had happened during that day with Dad. 'Hmm, it seems Dad has changed, Oliver.' I pulled his button nose. 'How can he have said that all women are the same? I mean, I don't think that all men are the same. I don't see Dad in the same way I see Ian, and then I don't see Jamal in the same way I see Beacon Wallis.' I smiled to myself. That really goes without saying.

I wondered what could've happened in the restaurant while I was in the loo.

It had surprised me that Dad held such narrow-minded views about women. Now I remembered that from time to time Mum had dropped little hints about how I would soon find out about my dad. I used to put it down to Mum just having a dig at Dad, but now I had to admit that some of the things she said must've been true. I thought of the way Dad hadn't believed me when I said that I had seen Marlene coming out of the steak house with a man. It upset me that he took her word instead of mine. It was so unbelievable when Colin had come into the restaurant. Hmm, I think I'll have to go to church this Sunday.

I knew that sooner or later I would have to tell Mama Tiny what had happened, and wondered how she would react. And Mum – I felt as though I had let her down in not believing some of the things she had said about Dad, not that they were that terrible, but made him seem insensitive to the fact that women were human beings.

Mum had always said that Dad hadn't liked her working in an office, probably because in his office some of the women – married and single – used to get a bit drunk at lunchtime and couldn't do their work when they came back, and just laughed and acted stupid. Mum said that whenever there was an office party Dad was disgusted at the way the women made it obvious that they fancied him or the other men. She had told Dad time and again that her office was different, but even after meeting some of the other women there he still felt the same way. Mum thought that Dad hadn't minded when the women paid him attention, but couldn't stand the thought that Mum might easily find herself in that position.

That's what I found so hard to believe. Dad knew that Mum was nothing like that yet it was as though he didn't trust her. I had thought all along that Dad really looked up to Mum and put her in a different class, above most women. I remembered the time Dad and I were down the West End shopping for me (which was nice) and there were these two girls in front of us with mini skirts on and wigs (trying to look like Mel and Kim, but they just couldn't carry it off). All the men were looking at them, and they were getting dirty looks from women.

I gave Dad a sidelong glance to see what he was doing, and he said, 'Those girls are just looking for men to pick them up. Look at the state of them. Your mum has a better figure than them any day.' I felt really chuffed. That was the sort of answer that I had wanted from him.

When I got home and told Mum, she said, 'The reason your dad said that about those girls was either because he must've known girls like them and knew what sort they were, or he is just being his usual critical self, and is it only now that your Dad has noticed my figure. He's never said anything before. When we were together he was forever saying that I should go on a diet, that I'm overweight and shouldn't let myself go, that it was embarrassing for him as my husband for me to be that size. He is such a hypocrite. Hmm, you'll see.' She banged my plate down on the table so hard (she was serving dinner) that the gravy spilled all over my skirt.

At the time, I just thought that Mum was a little jealous of Dad taking me to the West End shopping, or perhaps she hadn't heard him properly and had misunderstood him. I just didn't see my dad then how Mum did. Hmm.

Now, as I lay in bed, I realised that Mum must've been right in all those little things she used to say about him. I always knew that Dad was not perfect, but it made me wonder if he had been showing me his 'best' side all along, and that was why I couldn't find any fault with him. Now he had let it slip and my eyes were open.

I remembered Patrice saying that I had been the cause of my parents' break-up. I knew now that this was untrue: it was between them, and had nothing to do with me. What a mess!

My room was getting lighter. I looked at my watch on the table – 5.45. 'Is that all? Well, good night, Oliver.' I blew MJ a kiss and all of a sudden tiredness washed over me. I turned off the light and rolled over.

Twelve

Janeese and I both sat on the window ledge in my room looking out on to the garden.

'Your mum must have green fingers,' Janeese said, with her nose pressed against the window-pane.

'Yeah, she's always in the garden doing something or other to it. I think it's boring pulling up weeds and planting things.' Janeese breathed on the window to mist it up and drew a face.

'How can you say it's boring if you haven't tried. It's

hard work and you can do your back in. Besides, look at the end result, that's the main thing. Sometimes you do something not for the immediate result, but the rewards that come after a time.' She rubbed out the face.

We both sat there staring out of the window.

'Your mum works really hard, you know,' said Janeese.

'Yeah, I know, but I help her too.'

'I don't just mean around the house and that, I mean the fact that she runs the house all on her own, looks after you and . . .'

'Hold on, I'm a big girl now, I don't need looking after,' I said.

'You're not understanding me, Kiesha, you're just jumping down my throat. What I'm trying to say is, for a woman on her own, you mum has done all right. She holds down a job, runs a house, a car, and all those sort of things. It just makes me think that perhaps one day my mum might be in the same position as your mum and I want to be able to help her as much as I can.'

I couldn't answer that. I knew what Janeese had said was true.

She lay down on my bed, with her head at the foot and her feet at the head. 'Kiesha,' she looked at me, 'how's your dad?'

I cupped my face between my hands (it helped me to think). I didn't know what to say at first, I didn't fancy talking about what had happened in the restaurant.

'Well? What's happened?' said Janeese impatiently.

'Er, not much.'

'Is that all you can say? I thought you had something on your mind you wanted to tell me, that's all.'

'No, there's nothing more to it than that. I saw him last Saturday and he seemed his usual self.' I shrugged.

'So, how do you feel?' she probed.

I rolled my eyes to the ceiling, licked my top lip, scratched my head, shrugged my shoulders again. 'Okay.'

Janeese sighed. She sat up and faced me. 'I don't know why you're being all brave and "Look at me, I'm a martyr" for. Why don't you just tell me what's going on in your head, and get it out of your system?'

I began to tell her about Marlene and what had happened in the resturant. It just poured out. As I related it all to Janeese, I began to get really upset and feel sick, it was too much. When I'd finished, she never said a word. Time slipped by. The sun went in. The sky became overcast, which made the room gloomy. Janeese came and put her arm around me, I put my head on her shoulder. We sat there saying nothing.

The bathroom light was switched on and its light oozed its way under my door.

We parted, still in silence. We sort of knew that words would have spoilt that atmosphere.

I began searching in the bottom of my wardrobe.

'Look at this,' I said softly to Janeese, giving her a photo.

She switched on the bedside lamp and scrutinised the photo.

'It's your mum and dad on their wedding day.' She handed it back.

'It's a lie.' I held the photo to my chest and bent my head, rocking myself on the end of my bed.

'No, it's not a lie, it's just, it's just life. It seems that I'll soon be in the same boat as you and Beacon and all the other kids at school who live with only one parent. At least you have Mama Tiny,' said Janeese.

I looked at the photo again. 'But I want my parents to be together again. There's no reason why they shouldn't be. I know that Mum definitely loves Dad, and Dad said he loves Mum, so why can't they just make up and get together again and we can be a happy family?' I felt really helpless at not being successful in getting them back together. 'I've really tried to get them back together again.

148

I even saved up my pocket money to take Mum to the Pizza Hut and "accidentally" meet Dad there, but Mum sussed out that there was something fishy going on and Dad at the last minute called it off, he couldn't make it or something. Anyway, Mum and I still managed to go, but it wasn't the same.' I sniffed. I felt right choked.

'Sometimes it isn't a good idea to get people back together again once they've split up. Look, at least you're able to see them both. My mum and dad had a really big argument the other day, and lately they've been having them right in front of Neal and me, and Dad said from the day Mum and he split up, that's it, he never wants to see her or us again. Mum said that he shouldn't be hard on us kids, after all he is our dad, but he just ranted and raved.

'What does Neal feel about it all?'

'Well, Neal doesn't say too much. But then, he's always out, but I think it's because he can't stand the arguing. Perhaps it'll be better if my parents part, at least there'll be peace and quiet in the house.'

I looked up at the picture of MJ on the wall and thought, at least he's got his animals, and sniffed.

'Kiesha and Janeese, come fi yu food,' shouted Mama Tiny from downstairs.

We both stood up and I put my dark glasses on. 'How do I look, Janeese?' I said.

She laughed. 'You look a superstar now.' We both went downstairs.

When we were sitting around the table I could see Mama Tiny and Mum looking at each other and then at me. They couldn't see me properly because my glasses were mirror ones, but I could see them.

I leant over my plate, which was a wrong move, because the steam from the soup misted up my glasses and I couldn't see what I was eating, so I took my glasses off.

'What wrong chile?' asked Mama Tiny, looking worried.

'I can't see my soup bowl; the steam clouded up my glasses.'

'Well, mi glad yu tek off de eye glass,' she said.

Mum put her spoon down, 'Okay, let's have it out. What's the matter?'

All eyes were on me. I wanted to say so much, but I didn't know where to start. Thank goodness for Janeese, she more or less said it for me.

'Er, I think I know why Kiesha has been crying. You see, she's upset about her dad and you, Mrs Ferell, not getting back together, because she so much wants you to be together again, and she now realises that it isn't going to happen, and it's made her unhappy,' she finished in a whisper.

Nobody said anything at first and then we all seemed to start at once.

'Kiesha, I didn't realise you were still so upset about your dad and me. I'm so sorry,' said Mum.

'Hmm hmm, de chile must miss her fadda,' said Mama Tiny, spooning some soup into her mouth.

I just shrugged: 'It would've been nice if you were together again.'

Just before I went to bed, Mum called me into her room, looking sad. I sat on the edge of her bed next to her.

'Kiesha, how do you feel now?'

I kept my head down and shrugged. 'I don't know,' I said in all honesty.

'Well, you're a big girl now, or should I say a young woman? What has happened to your dad and me was a fact of life. Even though I love your dad, perhaps not in the same why I did when we were first together –' she paused and looked thoughtful. 'I do feel that your dad loves me in his own way, but if we were to come together again, I don't think it would work. Our love would become destructive and it wouldn't be good for either of us and you would most certainly suffer.' She looked at me to see if I understood what she was saying.

'But Mum, if you both love one another, I can't see what the problem is. I could understand it if you hated each other, but you don't. Oh, it's so confusing,' I cried.

She stretched out her hand and stroked my face. I could see that she wanted to say so much to me, but somehow she just couldn't.

'Mum, what do you want to tell me about Dad?'

She looked at the floor and I could sense that she was trying to sort out in her mind the right words to use.

'Kiesha, your dad,' she looked at me, 'is basically very selfish, and where women are concerned he has some very strange ideas. He is a very jealous man.'

'But what exactly has he done?' I asked.

She signed. 'What hasn't he done?' she said almost to herself. 'Look, okay. Your dad wasn't a bad provider. He could be quite loving when *he* felt like it. Yes, that's one of his problems: he loves loving when he feels like it and with whom he likes, and he thinks that I'm doing the same thing. It was so unbearable living with him.'

I knew, from Marlene, what Mum was trying to say, but I wasn't sure I wanted to hear it. The thought of my dad with other women while he was with my mum was hard to take in. Why would he want other women? I couldn't understand it.

I noticed a horrible sensation, starting somewhere around my belly-button, like a gnawing ache, that spread slowly right across my stomach and made me feel a bit sick. The funny thing was that I didn't want to cry. I felt as though I had cried enough to last me a lifetime. A strange thing was happening to me: I felt different, as though I had come into the real world, with a few starts and stops and finally with a bump. So this is what being grown-up is all about. Pain, suffering, humiliation, finding out things about people that surprise, if not shock you.

I sat on the edge of the bed, it could've been the edge of the world. I looked at my hands in my lap: they looked the same. I wriggled my toes in my slippers: they were all there. I breathed in and then out: everything working okay. Well, what could've happened?

'You're quiet, Kiesha. You sure you're okay?' said Mum, creasing her eyebrows.

'Yeah, fine. I just find it all a little strange, that's all. I never knew that Dad was like that. I must've been going around with blinkers on, not to have noticed that something was wrong between you. What I mean to say is that you never argued or had fights. It shocked me so much that you were splitting up, I couldn't understand why, and then when you did, I wondered if I was to blame. It was a horrible feeling not knowing.' I shrugged.

'No, darling, it wasn't your fault at all, you must never think that. To tell you the truth, if it wasn't for the fact that you were around we would have split up sooner.'

Janeese's snoring was keeping me awake, but the truth was I couldn't sleep because I felt as though Dad had betrayed Mum and me. What had driven him into the arms of other women? The thought was giving me a headache.

I tried to think back to those mornings when I would go into their bedroom and it looked as though Dad had either gone out early, or he hadn't come home yet. Whenever I asked Mum where he was she would say something or other, not really making much sense to me sometimes, but she didn't appear to be bothered, so I never worried much either. Now I could see that he was out with 'someone'.

I wondered if all men were like this. What a horrible thought! Was my dad one of many or one of a few? Well, that's it. I'm not getting married. I don't even think I want a boyfriend. I thought about what Janeese had said about Neal. If he was anything like her dad, it would be a nightmare for any woman unlucky enough to end up with him!

When I think about it seriously, relationships are really hard. To spend your life with someone for ever, doing things with them and for them, especially when you don't want to do it, and you have kids as well, oh, no, that would be terrible. I thought about all the kids at my school whose parents were separated and it suddenly occurred to me that it was the women that were left with the children – and all the hassle, I might add. How did that work out then? I wondered. Where did all the men go? Did any of the children go with their dads? How much help did the dads give their women who were left with the children? Did they still provide for them even after they had gone? What a hard life!

Janeese was downstairs washing the breakfast things with Mama Tiny. She seemed so happy staying here for a couple of nights and it was good going to school together. It must be such a break for her to be away from home since her parents are always attacking one another, poor thing. I'll tell her she can stay whenever she wants. In a way I was glad that school was finishing soon. During the holiday Janeese would be able to stay here as much as she wanted. I did feel different, as though I now saw people and things in different colours, it was strange.

Tidying up my wardrobe and my drawers, I came across the photo album with pictures of me when I was young (well, younger than now). I flicked through the pages – some of them were so funny. Then I took out the picture I'd shown Janeese of Mum and Dad's wedding day. They looked so young and there was an air almost of innocence about them, just like young children have. Dad looked really pleased, Mum happy.

It seemed wrong, somehow, having the photo. Had what I said to Janeese last night, about the wedding being a lie, been true? I thought it was supposed to be until death do us part. Well, that's what they said whenever there was a wedding on the telly.

I ran my fingers over the glossy finish on the photo. What a shame. I was too sad to cry, but the pain was heavy inside me. I picked up the scissors from the bedside table and carefully cut the photo down the middle.

I had Dad in my left hand and Mum in my right. I looked from one to the other. They were almost like strangers to each other. My parents. I placed them in the album on different pages and put it away at the bottom of the wardrobe. That was where it belonged.

'Well, what do you reckon, MJ?' He smiled at me and I guessed he would say something like, 'You've got yourself together baby.' He could probably make that line into a mega hit. I'm sure his eye twinkled!

'And what do you think Oliver?' I smiled at my teddy bear. He looked at me with his glass eyes and they were smiling too.

Well, life has to go on, time stops for no one, not even me, I said to myself.

I looked up at MJ on the wall and said in my best Lady Di voice, 'Hmm, I think it's better for both of us that we wait until I at least finish my exams and then, of course, reach the age of consent. I'll do some travelling the world with my friends, have a boyfriend or two (just to test the waters, you understand), save some money (Mama Tiny says that 'Every ooman should ave money put down, an dem nar fi leave everyting up to dem man' – wise advice I think!) and generally sort myself out, before we tie the knot, or jump the broomstick or run off to Gretna Green.'

I opened my window to let in the fresh morning air. I breathed deeply and I could really feel the air filling up my lungs. It was great.

Janeese was in the garden. 'Come on down, the price is right,' she laughed, waving the shovel in her hand.

I waved back, laughing along with her.

154